MW00892403

A Beach Dweller.

Chapter 1 ------ An awakening --------- Page 1.

Chapter 2 ------ The Tutor --------- Page 5.

Chapter 3 ------ A Foolish Girl ---------- Page 10.

Chapter 4 ------ Joey has Parents? ---------- Page 15.

Chapter 5 ------ A failed Seduction---------- Page 21.

Chapter 6 ------ Ashley the Woman ------ Page 27.

Chapter 7 ------ My competition ---------- Page 30.

Chapter 8 ------ The suspect ---------- Page 34.

Chapter 9 ------ Our first adventure---------- Page 36.

Chapter 10 ----- A Love interest --------- Page 41.

Chapter 11 ------ My protector ---------- Page 43.

Chapter 12 ------ A Lost Love ---------- Page 45.

Chapter 13------ Life Continues -------- Page 47.

Chapter 14 ------ Candy's surprise---------- Page 50.

Chapter 15 ------ A step back--------- Page 53.

Chapter 16 ------- Self Inflicted --------- Page 56.

Chapter 17 ------ The seductress ---------- Page 58.

Chapter 18 ------- A Girl's Reputation----- Page 60.

Chapter 19 ------ A confusion---------- Page 61.

Chapter 20 ------ Lost Love, New Love ---- Page 66.

Chapter 21 ------ Alone again ---------- Page 68.

Chapter 22 ------ A Happy Finale---------- Page 69.

Chapter 23 ------ De-Jar-Vu ---------- Page 71.

Chapter 24 ------ Realization --------- Page 74.

Chapter 1.
An awakening.

I was always just a young girl who drifted along enjoying life, not putting too much effort into life except that I tried to amuse myself wherever possible. When I was in high school, my parents moved to a seaside village just as I was starting year eleven at school. My grades had always been average, and it was only now that I realized that average grades were never going to allow me to go to university, and so now for the first time in my entire life, I had decided that I needed to put extra effort into my schoolwork. I decided that if I could make it to university, then I would mix with people going somewhere and would hopefully attract an intelligent husband in order that we start a family and would live comfortably ever after.

I had the same dreams as did most girls, I suppose, and that was to wake up in the morning with a loving handsome young man beside me. Of course, dreams are but dreams and every morning I woke up alone. I was smart enough to realize that girls are attracted to boys in their environment and if I were to have a chance to meet up with a boy with a future, then I would have to be able to attend a university where my chances for meeting such a young man would be more probable.

All plans come adrift at some time and so did mine. I tried to study harder, which I did with less than amazing results. I tried to keep fit, which I did by jogging every morning, just after daylight in the summer and before daylight in the winter. I would run from my house down to the beach and would run along the hard sand which was found just above the waterline.

I believed what people told me, that one had to have a sound body to have a sound mind. I had a sound body, but my mind was apparently not sound enough to achieve an increase in my scholastic abilities. For many days in a row, as I would be jogging along the waterline, I would see what seemed to be a sleeping bag in the soft sand near the dunes with something or someone under it, or in it, as from time to time it moved ever so slightly.

My curiosity finally got the better of me and so I walked into the soft sand where I could investigate as to what was in the bag. To my amazement it was a teenage boy not much older than myself who had obviously slept there during the night. I stood beside him, bent over while looking into his eyes which were shut until he opened them, and in a sleepy haze said, "Good morning".

I jolted back away from him as I was perhaps a little apprehensive, after which I realized that he was again asleep. I walked down to the hard sand near the water's edge and continued jogging while thinking of how down and out a person would need to be, to have to sleep in the soft sand on the beach at night. I also thought of how visually appealing he seemed to me and how his eyes seemed to look through me. Even though this beach dwelling boy appealed to me, I was aware that I should stay clear of him as I had a goal which was to meet a successful partner in life, and I was sure that such a person would not be found sleeping on the beach at night.

The following days, I would run past looking at the boy snoozing away until I could bear my curiosity no longer, and, on my return, when I found him in a sitting position taking in the morning sun, I stopped beside him and sat down, attempting to make conversation. I had no idea why I would do such a thing, but it was as if my destiny demanded it. I had my future planned and it surely would not happen in the way I planned if I were to associate with who I considered to be a down and out beach dweller, what most people refer to as beach-bums.

I said that my name was Ashleigh and he replied that his name was Joey. Soon after the standard chit chat was over, I asked why he slept on the beach, to which he replied, "The sand is much softer than a park bench".

I immediately asked, "Don't you have a home?" Joey then smiled as he replied, "You are sitting in my lounge room this very minute." I was in shock that someone my age would be homeless and living down at the beach and so I continued with, "What school do you attend?" This question seemed to amuse Joey as he answered, "I have not attended school since year seven in primary school and have no intention of going back again in the near future, even if pretty girls like you are in abundance at school." I only smiled a reply as I did not want the conversation going down this track.

Joey was a handsome boy and if he would have had at least attended school and had some ambition, then I would perhaps have continued our conversation. I had ambitions for myself, and to associate with the likes of Joey, I knew, would not pay dividends for my own future. I told him that I needed to continue with my run, in order that I would arrive at school before it started, and so did.

During the day at school, I could not get Joey out of my mind. I could not imagine how someone could function in society without attending school, and yet he sounded very articulate for someone who I would categorize as a no-hoper, going nowhere fast. Females are by nature curious individuals and so I had no other option than to find out how a boy or young man could exist on the beach without proper schooling.

The next day was Saturday, which I would usually spend at some beach or another, but this Saturday I decided to go to our local beach as I thought that I might run into Joey and find out more about him. I arrived late on Saturday only to find other girls who I knew, sitting on their towels. I sat down with them and chatted with the meaningless banter which girls seem to be proficient at. During this chit chat I looked at a group of slightly older boys standing with their surfboards and recognized Joey amongst them. I asked the girls if they were aware who the tanned boy was standing chatting with the others.

They all seemed to know Joey or mainly knew about him. They said that he mostly lived in a dilapidated old shack that backed onto the sandy beach; seemed to have no steady job and never attended any school that they knew of. They smiled as they said that any girl who was not too concerned with keeping her virtue could go and chat to him as he would only be too willing to take it from her. It appeared as if the girls were making fun of me because I enquired about him.

When I was younger, I was very much attached to my virtue, but the older I became, the less important it seemed to me, but I would never consider giving it to a no-hoper like Joey. Joey had seemed harmless and well-spoken for an illiterate young man, and to the complete surprise of the other girls, I stood and walked over to Joey and began to chat with him, "Hello Joey, you must have left the tap on in your bathroom as water is coming into your living room." Joey smiled at my attempt at humor and said that I looked even better in my swimmers than I did in my joggers.

I was wise to the ways of older boys and young men and realized why a self-serving compliment was often bestowed on an older girl or young woman, but I still had no objections to it. The surf was such that no self-respecting surfer would venture out to catch a wave and so Joey asked me if I cared to share a milkshake with him. I was trying to solve the mystery as to what he meant by sharing. Perhaps a milkshake with two straws, and then the question was as to who would be expected to pay for the milkshake in the first place. I walked to the milk-bar with Joey, after which we were soon sitting in a cubicle when Joey said, "I prefer chocolate. Which would you prefer?"

I was thinking that I should say chocolate so we could share, but finally said, "I like strawberry." I looked into Joey's eyes, questioning him without asking who would be expected to stand up to order and pay for the milkshakes. Joey finally stood and walked behind the counter and took two containers and made both our shakes for us. After they were made, Joey made no attempt to pay for them and came back to me.

I was appalled, as I thought that he must have a stand-over relationship with the employees as not one questioned him regarding the making of and the taking of the milkshakes without paying for them. I considered that they must be afraid of him, and so, let him be.

I immediately asked, "Why did you walk behind the counter like you owned the place and not paid for the milkshakes. Joey just smiled as he seemed to speak down to me, "Beach-bums don't have to pay when they have a deal with the owner. I am on call when they are overly busy, and I come down to help them out for free. I do not receive money for this, but they allow me to have breakfast here every day and the odd milkshake if I am with a pretty girl like yourself."

I smiled at Joey as I thought that this was very clever for an uneducated boy with only grade seven education. I asked Joey why he had dropped out of school to which he replied, "When I was finished year seven at school and my parents were having a birthday party for me, I had met a young girl down the beach who was paying attention to my advances and so I decided that it may well be more beneficial for me to stay with her than attend my own birthday party. When my father came down to the beach looking for why I had failed to attend my own birthday party, I told him that I planned to stay down at the beach with this appreciative girl. He stated in no uncertain terms that if I did not come home there and then, then not to bother coming home at all and I should pack up and move out. Well, my dear Ashleigh, the girl went home that night when her parents called for her, and I am still here living on the beach."

I didn't know whether to laugh or cry and so said nothing. I then explained that I heard from the other girls that he lived in a house on the water's edge. Joey continued with his story, "After my father threw me out, mother said that I could live in a room in a rental shack that she owned down on the beach as long as I organized tenants for the other rooms and kept them in check."

I then asked, "And why then did I find you sleeping in the sand." Joey then gave me a mischievous smile as he replied, "I rented out my own room to two females who I thought would have no objection to me sharing the room, but I was badly mistaken, and so I have had to spend two weeks on the beach. I often rent out all the other rooms, and the income from them goes to my mother, but when I rent out my own room then I can keep that money."

I was amazed at this cunning uneducated boy, in that he had managed to survive all this time and seemed happy with little future for himself. After conversing with Joey, I felt that I was being seduced by his cunning smile. Such a relationship was not what I wanted for myself, as my priorities were to improve my grades and attempt to be accepted into a university where I would mix with ambitious people with a future.

That night in bed, I could think of nothing other than Joey, handsome, articulate, uneducated, but seductive, Joey. My puberty years were behind me and so such thoughts were always on my mind. That night I held Joey close and let him do ungentlemanly things to me. In dreams, a girl can do much more than when she is awake as the next day the slate will be wiped clean again and a night of passion will be no more than a memory, if that.

I continued jogging every morning but perhaps a little earlier so that I could talk with Joey as the sun came up over the horizon. The more I spoke to Joey the more knowledgeable I found him. This was a mystery to me, and another mystery was why I enjoyed talking to a beach dweller with no future or hope for betterment of himself. One morning as Joey sat up in his sleeping bag, I was not immediately aware of whether he was wearing any boxer shorts which he normally wore or had slept naked.

Being the age that I was, I followed the contours of his body into his sleeping bag to find that he not only was wearing his boxer shorts but had a headlamp with three books tucked in beside him. Joey saw my eyes staring at what they should not, so I immediately asked about the books trying to distract attention from what my eyes were trying to uncover. Joey replied that he often read books at night before going to sleep.

A beach dwelling boy reading books seemed like an incompatibility. I thought that Girlie magazines would have been the extent of a beach-bums interest, but these books were intellectually stimulating and intellectually above the literature that I would attempt to read myself. Were these books to impress me? Perhaps Joey wanted my opinion of him to attain a higher level. Did it show that I looked down on this beach dwelling boy? I have to admit that I was attracted to Joey but my interacting with him was only to satisfy a curiosity in myself.

I tried to tell myself that this was the only reason I comtinued talking with Joey but deep down I knew that I was fooling myself, even though I would never consider having a relationship with a beach dweller such as Joey.

I realized that I wanted to kiss Joey, perhaps even to embrace him, perhaps even slip into his sleeping bag with him. What was I thinking, as I had my future planned, and even though I was having difficulty in getting good grades to allow me to go to university, I hoped for such things to be possible. At university I would meet a handsome intelligent young man who would have a future and who I would have children with and who would definitely not have to end up sleeping on the beach.

In order to have a future, I would have to use my brain instead of my girlish libido and distance myself from Joey. I looked at Joey one last time and decided to distance myself from him. Perhaps I would dream of Joey at night knowing that dreams are very forgiving, and no consequences would have to be faced the following morning.

I was soon back at school trying to better myself with little success. One day when I was at home studying my little heart out, mum and dad came into my room and both sat on my bed and explained to me that if I wanted to receive tutoring, then they would be willing to pay for it. I needed tutoring badly but did not wish to ask my parents as that would be a financial burden on them, but now they were offering.

I replied that I would love to be tutored if we could afford it. Father then explained that other parents had highly recommended a particular tutor and said that he had improved the grades of their sons and daughters; some into A grade students. They said that this person guaranteed at least B+ results in one subject otherwise there would be no charge. I was over the moon as I was In dire need of tuition as all my extra study had as yet, amounted to zip.

I imagined my tutor to be perhaps an older retired teacher or a lady with older children who had grown but needed some extra monies on the side. I had no concept as to what was in store for me.

Chapter 2.
The Tutor.

I arrived home from school on Monday afternoon only to find Joey waiting on my doorstep. I was confused as to why Joey would take the time to pursue me as he had the reputation of being a less than a monogamist person, with a selection of girls seeking his company and so why would he pursue me? I asked why he was there which seemed to confuse him. After a moment of silence he replied, "I have come to tutor a pretty but dumb young girl that goes by the name of Ashleigh. Do you know of her or as to where she may be?"

I smiled at his attempt at humor but was dumbfounded as to how Joey would show up to tutor me, as I was aware that Joey was a beach-bum who never went past year seven at school. I was about to send him on his way but was reluctant as I was a girl who liked his company, and after all, this could be quite amusing as he would not charge my parents unless I received a B+.

We were soon in my room where I already had an extra chair placed ready for my tutor. As soon as we were both seated, I asked what type of scam he was pulling as he could not possibly be a tutor for students in their senior years. I asked for an explanation, and he said that all was kosher and that we should start immediately.

I was wary of inviting him into my bedroom where he may have wished to take liberties with me. Would I mind if he did take liberties with me? I had dreamt about that very thing the previous night but today was reality and now I would have to think with my brain instead of my girlish libido. I decided to take him upstairs to my bedroom where I studied, as my parents would soon be home, which would limit any forwardness on his part.

My worst subject was Mathematics B and so I said that we should start there. I smiled as I gave him my textbook which he had asked for. I expected the look of fear on Joey's features when he opened the book, but he began to read and asked if I would make him a cup of tea.

I soon returned to my room with his cup of tea, only to find Joey reading the central chapters of my book. flicking through the pages faster than I have ever seen anyone do. I wanted to learn, and I had tried all other options and so I thought that I would humor him. Joey then told me to lay on my bed and to close my eyes. This was what I had expected of Joey who immediately began to speak asking me relevant and irrelevant questions. I seemed to be quickly answering questions following his lead until he said to undo the top buttons of my blouse. I had already undone two buttons before I realized what I was doing.

I sat up and asked, "What are you doing?" Joey then smiled as he replied, "I am trying to make you think and not to blindly accept what has been told you without thinking. School teachers will tell you to read and read, and read some more, but you must think in between, otherwise all that reading will appear like a dream and exist only in your short-term memory. I will teach you how to put this knowledge straight into your long-term memory." Joey then smiled as he continued, "And there is no need to redo the buttons on your blouse unless you think it inappropriate to have them undone."

I returned his smile as I immediately redid the buttons on my blouse, but fully understood that I had been blindly following his lead without thinking, which made me recall just how many times that I had read a full page of writing in a novel only to have no recollection of what I had just finished reading only seconds before. Embarrassed by what I had done, I redid my buttons, all the while realizing that I liked the thought of exposing myself to a young man and to feel his reaction which of course would have to be my own reaction as I received little from Joey.

Joey and I had been at it for a full hour when father knocked and then entered my room. Father was furious when he saw Joey and said in no uncertain terms that I was not allowed to have boys in my room. I quickly explained that Joey was my tutor which was not believed at first, but then father asked, "And what are your credentials son?"

Joey then replied, "Mr. Jackson, Ashleigh's teachers have credentials and yet her results are more than just a little disappointing. I believe that you have employed me on recommendations from your acquaintances and so the question of my credentials is now moot." I had never heard anyone speak so forcefully and so eloquently to my father like that before. My father then looked at the floor for a moment and replied, "All right then. Just make sure that the door to Ashley's bedroom stays open when you are here."

Joey left and soon after, father commented, "This young tutor comes highly recommended and so we will persevere, as after all, we have little to lose." I hugged my father who then left the room after which I lay on my bed contemplating what had just happened to me. An almost homeless boy with year seven education was teaching me, a year eleven student, to improve her grades. The realities of this seemed beyond my comprehension. I had discarded a handsome homeless beach dwelling boy who I had met sleeping on the beach, who had been living there since just after his year-seven at school had finished, only to find him tutoring me.

How could such a boy have the schooling-plus intellect to handle such a task. I had to find out and so that night I told my parents that I would be jogging down to the beach and sitting for a while enjoying the cool breeze and then returning. This was not unusual at all as I often did exactly that, and so I was permitted to go. Normally I would put on any clean pair of running shorts but now for a reason I was trying hard to understand, my selection took some consideration. Usually, I would wear a tee-shirt but this day I wore a colored singlet with a low front. Of course, I knew why I did such a thing as I hoped to impress Joey, even though I wanted nothing to do with him.

As soon as I reached the waterline, I tried to find Joey, but he was not there. I then walked to the milk-bar and found him sitting in a cubicle reading a book. I slid in opposite him which surprised him momentarily but then he adjusted, saying, "I have apparently had a Florence Nightingale effect on you, and you have sought me out." I asked what a 'Florence Nightingale' effect was, to which he replied, "That is when a patient falls in love with his nurse or doctor, or in this case in that a student falls in love with his or her teacher."

I laughed at his statement even though there was possibly some truth in it, but I was there because I was as curious as I had ever been. I wanted to know more about him and so I asked him to explain how an uneducated teenager could be instructing students who obviously had a greater education than he himself did.

I sat waiting until he began, "Knowledge is gained by reading the experiences and ideas of others, and if you are interested and pay attention, it is then easy to retain that knowledge. I like reading and am interested in most facets of life and so I have good retention of everything that I read."

I asked Joey if his results were good in year seven, prompting him to continue. Joey replied, "I had always had top marks during my younger years but was infuriated by the repetition of everything, over and over again. I thought that school was a drag, and I was often ostracized for reading a non-related book during class. I was, however, given some slack, as my results were beyond reproach. I have read many or perhaps all of the schoolbooks that you have and perhaps have a greater interest of what is contained in them than yourself, and certainly a greater retention of what is written inside of them."

Joey smiled before he continued, "My dear Ashley, let me just say that it is socially unacceptable for a teacher to form a relationship with a pupil, and so if you wish to sleep with me you will have to wait until I am finished teaching you, and only then will I allow you to share my bed."

I was totally incensed that he spoke to me in such a way, even though, he was a handsome boy, and I was a girl who was just over her puberty years and thought about such things constantly. I had thoughts of slapping his face, but as if he had read my mind, he pushed his frame back onto the bench seat of the cubicle, creating too much distance to allow me to do so.

I wanted a reprisal to such an assumption even though it may well be true. Was this chap a mind reader? How did he know that I wanted to slap him?

I asked, "Are all your relatives as uneducated and abrupt as you are?" Joey explained that most of his family were well educated people except for his grandmother who only had three years of schooling but was perhaps the most knowledgeable of all his family. She had guided him during his younger years and instilled in him that all knowledge could be found by simply reading books and had taught him to read before he had even done one day of schooling.

I realized that I was in the presence of a miracle, not my miracle I was sad to say, but a strange one and a handsome one too boot. I jogged home to find my parents there, asking inquisitively as to what had taken me so long. I explained that I had seen my tutor in a milk bar while jogging past and had sat talking with him in the cubicle and had quizzed him as to how he had become a tutor.

I explained most of what I knew, except for the parts that no parent should hear from their post puberty daughter. They were amazed, in that he had seemingly no education at all but was successful in tutoring others. I was amazed myself but had trouble placing such a background in with a boy whose main objectives in life, it seemed, were bedding as many young women as possible while living on the beach where there was no absence of young women to choose from, (if the statements of the other girls were to be believed).

That night after I had fallen into a deep sleep, I again found Joey on the beach in his sleeping bag but this time as I jogged passed, I slid into his sleeping bag where he turned me into a woman many times over. Luckily, the next morning I awoke to find that I was still virtuous and that it had been only a dream.

Life continued for me, and Mondays and Thursdays I would look forward to spending time with Joey as I had madly fallen in love with him, even though it seemed to be a one-sided affair. I always sat uncomfortably close to Joey who usually moved his frame away from me if the space permitted him to do so.

My thoughts not always concentrated on my study material but drifted as to why Joey seemed to pay me little attention in a sensual way. I knew that I was not completely hideous and had received much unwanted attention in the past from other boys and so it was a mystery to me as to why I did not seem to appeal to Joey at all.

I finally had had enough and in a fit of desperation I spoke to Joey with an agitated voice, "Do I have to remove all of my clothing and jump on top of you before you pay me even the slightest attention?" Joey only smiled, "My dear, dear Ashleigh, as pleasing as that sounds to me, we must continue on our pathway for you to achieve better term results, but as an incentive for you to look forward to, I will take you to supper and to see a movie if you get B+ results in at least three of your subjects."

I considered that was the shallowest of statements, as even though I seemed to be improving out of sight, I was never going to get a B+ in any of my subjects, especially B+ in three of them. I had never had a B+ in my entire life and some uneducated tutor was never going to make that happen. I had many boys offer to take me to a movie previously, most of which were handsome and the odd one even had a grip on the English language and could speak coherently without difficulty, but never one who I wished to have accompany me as much as I did with Joey.

I now had a handsome boy who although being a beach bum, held my heart in his hands, but I would have to obtain results in my end term tests that were beyond me to even contemplate being successful at. I would, however, do my best, as the carrot dangling in front of me was too great to resist.

I could not understand how familiar Joey would be with me at times and yet at other times keep his distance. One day when I was seeing him to the door with my father being present, Joey bid me goodbye and kissed my cheek to the consternation of my father, even though my father said nothing. I would have preferred it if Joey had done so in the relative privacy of my room so that I could have improved his aim and responded, but while there, he always kept his distance from me.

Exams were coming up and I was lying on my bed reading a Mills and Boon book which had little to do with my education but which I enjoyed. I put my book down and at once realized what had been oblivious to me. Without a formal education there would be no possibility for Joey to ever make anything of himself and so his future looked bleak. I needed to know what Joey was planning for in the years to come and see if I could persuade him to see reason and get a formal education.

I sat for a while with the mental picture of three sleeping bags on the beach, one for Joey and myself and two smaller ones for our children. This was not my idea of how I wanted my life to turn out. I loved Joey but not so much that I would become a beach dweller myself and bring children into such an environment.

I put on my jogging outfit and jogged down to the beach and then to the milk bar but to no avail as he was nowhere to be found. I decided to go down to his house, which meant that if anyone saw me, it would mean that I would seem like another notch on his wall, another deflowered virgin whose reputation would be tarnished beyond repair.

I realized that my reputation would be in tatters if I were to be seen entering his male dominated beach house and yet I decided that my quest could not wait. I arrived at the house to find four young men sitting on the porch wearing boardshorts looking at the ocean and so I asked which room belonged to Joey after which they indicated which room. I knocked on the door and to my complete horror, the door was opened by a girl wearing the shortest of denim shorts with a tight top which housed a formidable shapely bosom that I was instantly envious of.

As the door swung open, my eyes gazed at Joey laying on his bed wearing only his swimmers. I knew what a reputation Joey had, and I should have known better than to arrive at his home unannounced. I was hurt and could think of nothing else to do but run away, which I did. I ran as fast as I could and almost made it to the hard sand but was tackled from behind by Joey who was quickly followed by the girl in the denim shorts.

Chapter 3.
A Foolish Girl.

This girl was laughing at me, which made me feel like a naive girl who had fallen in love with her teacher and had made a complete fool of herself. Joey ended up lying beside me, face down in the sand while this girl walked over and sat on Joey's back before she spoke to me, "You must be Ashleigh; Joey has told me much about you, as you have captured his very being."

Confused, I then asked, "And you must be his Wednesday girl then?" This girl then laughed at me as she replied "I am his forever-girl and have always been. I am his sister Susan." I was embarrassed by my girlish attitude but still managed a relieving smile by replying, "I am Ashleigh and am trying my best to relieve you of top position in his heart."

Susan smiled and then replied, "You have already done that, I believe." Joey lay on his stomach and with Susan still sitting on his back, and commented, "Get off me so that I can be part of this conversation about me." Susan then repositioned herself on the sand allowing Joey to sit up. Joey then asked, "And what could not wait until our next lesson?"

I replied, "I have just realized that you will have no future unless you do formal studies to be allowed into university to better yourself and without a formal education you will have no chance of doing that."

Susan then took over the conversation, "Ashleigh, you are thinking like the rest of humanity, but smarty-pants Joey is waiting until he is twenty-one years old and plans to enter university under the adult education criteria. He will then be able to sit for exams without the drudgery of having to sit through lecture upon lecture at university and mostly only doing the tests to achieve his ambitions." Susan then continued with a laugh as if she were to say something that was amusing," If that does not work for him, then he plans to go into politics as there is no requisite for any education at all in that field." We all laughed at the stupidity of it all, but it appeared that Joey had his present and his future all planned and under control.

Susan then left us, as she had come to see Joey but mostly to appraise the selection of young men to choose from, sitting on his verandah at that very moment.

Joey then looked into my eyes and spoke quietly to me, "And so my dear Ashleigh, you have been concerned about my future." I took a brave step by replying, "Not at all; I have been concerned about **our** future." I then asked about all the females that my friends had told me about, who had frequented his bed and whose virtue he had taken.

A smile moved across Joey's face, "Beautiful young women take men for granted. They believe that by having a seductive smile while wearing a shapely bikini, they can seduce any man on the planet. That may well mostly be the case, but some men require a woman to have at least some intellect and would never settle for anyone who could not get even one B+ in their end term results."

I wanted to hit him and yet wanted to hug and kiss him all at the same time, for I knew that he was doing all he could to better my chances in life by improving my scholastic results.

Did Joey think of me as the dumb girl who thought only of how to attract the opposite of her species by wearing a shapely bikini and having a cute smile, and if so, then how could I possibly change his opinion of me. I knew for a fact that many young men preferred seemingly dumb young women and so why would Joey be any different? I had never heard of a boy being attracted to a girl's intelligence but had received many a wolf whistle from a distance when I was out jogging in my shorty shorts. I considered that wearing my shorty shorts would not reflect my intellect from a distance and so that pathway of reasoning was now moot.

The end term tests were over, and I longed for the day when the results were to be placed on the notice board. Maybe if I achieved even one B+ then Joey would take me to dinner and a movie. I could only hope for such an outcome even though I knew that I had done better than ever before. I almost fell off my perch when viewing the notice board as I had achieved not only a B+ but another B and one A.

That Monday could not pass fast enough as I knew that Joey would be waiting for me to arrive home, and I was anticipating telling him of my end term results. As soon as I arrived home, I told Joey which movie I wanted to see but he said that I had achieved only one B+ and so did not achieve what we had agreed upon. I immediately attacked Joey with as much ferocity as I could muster from within myself but was no match for a lean muscular Joey who wrapped his arms around me, trapping my own arms beside my body.

As soon as Joey finished laughing, he looked into my eyes and without releasing his grip on me moved his face closer to me and kissed me. I was now in heaven and passionately returned his kiss when father and mother opened the door where they stood horrified by watching such an intimate act being portrayed by their normally reserved daughter. Joey paid the precarious situation no mind when he turned to my parents and exclaimed, "Two B's, one a B+ and one A."

It was only an instant later when my parents were involved in a four-way hug. As soon as we separated, I told my parents that I had a deal with Joey in that if I achieve three B+ results then he would take me to supper and a movie. My father, not thinking that I may well have some ulterior motive, commented, "Nonsense, I am shouting us all to a meal at any restaurant of your choosing."

This was not going exactly as I had envisaged, but at least I would be keeping company with Joey in the movie theatre after supper. I never drank alcohol and Joey only sipped on his glass of non-alcoholic wine and mother at her best was only good for one glass, while dear old dad made up for all our shortcomings. After our celebration, I found that my parents were even more pleased with my results than I was. Mother was forced to drive father home as he was in no state to drive home himself.

This left me with Joey who immediately grabbed my hand and asked, "What movie did you select for us to see?" I had selected what I had thought was a lovey-dovey movie which I thought would be in the Mills and Boon tradition, but I was soon in for a surprise.

I noticed that the movie had an R classification, but considered that nowadays, "What movie has not got such a classification?" I put down the armrest between our seats so I could snuggle up to Joey, but was soon regretting this action as the movie was a lot more explicit than in any of my Mills and Boon novels.

I was embarrassed and tried to distance myself from Joey but was trapped under his arm. I was annoyed by the selection of movie, as that may give the impression that I was a tramp and that it was my objective to seduce him by seeing such a movie. Joey pulled me closer every time that I tried to move away from him. I realized that a young girl has many conflicting tendencies as I wanted to distance myself from him and yet I wanted for him to tighten his embrace.

To say that the movie had no effect on me would be misleading as I wanted to do with Joey what was so explicitly shown on the movie screen. I felt safe as being in a crowded movie theatre, there was little chance of doing what was so blatantly portrayed for us on the screen. I was not so much afraid of Joey but more afraid of myself, as Joey seemed to have self-control with me and my self-control concerning Joey was still to be determined.

Totally embarrassed, I apologized for the movie, by admitting that I had taken little notice of the classification. Joey just smiled and said that a person could learn as much from watching a movie as reading a book and told me to pay attention, as I may have to refer to this movie's content if our relationship progressed further. I was embarrassed beyond belief as even though I had the same longings as any other young woman and knew that the result of preserving humanity was to engage in carnal acts, my conscious mind had not progressed past the holding of hands and a passionate kiss.

I had already dreamt of having Joey share my bed, but there was a long way between dreaming and acting on such dreams. I was already wanting to remove my clothing and Joey's and follow the exact plot of the movie if I may call it a plot. I was afraid of my own vulnerability and of what may well be expected of me. I realized that my predicament was caused by my own movie selection and so I had no one to blame except for myself.

The movie finally ended to my disappointment, as well as my relief. Before the lights again came on, Joey's hand found my waist creating an uncertainty in me, as I did not know where his hand wished to travel after that. Joey then pulled me to him and kissed me. I returned his kiss but not as forcefully as I was capable of, as under the circumstances, I did not wish to send him the wrong message.

On the way home, Joey drove me down to the beach where we spoke for hours and not once had he acted in any ungentlemanly manor except for a bit of kissing and cuddling.

As we were about to leave, I wondered why someone with a reputation of deflowering many young women would act so reservedly with me and so I asked him why. Joey smiled as he replied, "I have taught you to question everything, even what is written in non-fiction books and yet you do not even question the rantings of a group of young females who have nothing better to do than gossip about who is holding hands with who, who is kissing who, and who has lost their virtue to whoever."

Joey then continued as if he was giving me a lesson in life, "Things are seldom as they seem; an example would be found in Hollywood movies where a young man only has to kiss a girl once and the next thing is that she is pulling his hand towards a bedroom where they can perform the ultimate act. Your Mills and Boon novels are perhaps closer to reality than what you give them credit for.

Joey drove me home that night and gave me the customary hug and kiss before I exited his car. That night I realized that my life was now coming together more than I had ever dreamed of. I was achieving results at school which would in all probability allow me to go to university where I hoped to find a young man whose intellect would allow us to have a favorable future.

That had been my plan but as I was thinking these thoughts, I realized that the only person who I wanted to share my life could only be

Joey, a beach bum who I had found sleeping on a beach. All the aspirations which I had previously envisaged for my future were becoming unstuck.

What I did not immediately comprehend was that Joey's job with me was done and the following Monday when I arrived home, Joey was nowhere to be found. Realization had set in that I had been taught how to study and learn, and now there was nothing left for Joey to do, and the rest I would have to do myself. I had hoped that Joey would get in contact with me but realized that may not happen too soon.

I felt as all girls would feel, waiting for a call which I knew was not likely, from a boy who I wanted badly to have express his feelings for me, knowing that the first step in this direction would be a phone call. I would wait, as that is what society demanded, but was not at all happy with my situation.

The principal at my school, Ben Jacobs, wished to see me in his office as he thought that my improved results may be the product of cheating. After being given the third degree by my school principal, I explained that my parents had hired a tutor who had been responsible for my end term results and that he was a boy not much older than myself. I can still remember Mr. Jacobs question of me, "And what education and qualifications does this young man have?" I smiled as I replied, "Joey is an exceptional surfer but apart from that, has no formal education at all since terminating his education in year seven at this very school.

The principal replied, "I have heard of such gifted people but have never met one. I would be very pleased if I could meet with this young man." I smiled as I replied, "You will have to wait your turn as I would like to meet with him myself but have not seen him since he celebrated my end term results at a local restaurant with my parents and me. Mr. Jacobs only returned my smile, as I believe that he sensed that I was sweet on Joey. I was sweet on Joey of course but understood that it is the job of a male to pursue a female and not the other way around.

Time went on and I pined for Joey every day until such time that I decided that I would have to be the aggressor and chase after him. I still went jogging at the beach along the hard sand, always looking to see if someone was sleeping higher up in the soft sand. I did not wish to go to his house, full of young male surfers, as that would be pushing societies boundaries of my having any self-respect at all. I called in at the milk-bar only to find Susan sitting in a cubicle with a milkshake. As soon as I entered, Susan smiled and motioned me to come and sit with her.

As soon as our greetings were finalized, I asked where Joey was. Susan replied with no apparent regard to my feelings, by replying, "Joey has just returned from a month on Annabelle. I was hurt; I was horrified; I was appalled, and what did Susan mean by saying "**on** Annabelle". Did she mean some sexual connotation that I did not fully comprehend, or did she mean that their month away was paid for by Annabelle? As these questions were sending the neurons in my brain into overload, Susan said that Joey had phoned her on his return and asked her to meet him at the milk bar, and that she expected him to arrive at any moment. I wanted to get up and leave but before I could, Joey walked in the doorway and came to our cubicle and slid in beside me blocking any escape plan that I was considering.

As soon as his outer thighs and mine were tightly pushed together, Joey's hand reached for mine, but I pulled it away from him and asked, "And how is Annabelle?" Joey replied as if my query was of no consequence, "Annabelle was as sturdy as ever and she managed to survive the trip."

I could bear it no longer and tears were running down my cheeks like water does when running over the stones found under a waterfall. Both Susan and Joey looked at me with mouths slightly ajar, obviously not understanding why I was crying. Susan was the first to realize my plight and began to smile, "Ashleigh, are you aware that Annabelle is the name of a fishing trawler that Joey helps man when one of the crew is sick?"

It was then that I realized the error of my girlish conclusions and I believe that Joey realized them at the same time. He smiled as he placed his hand on my leg, just above the knee and squeezed.

Joey was in the process of removing his hand when I placed my hand on top of his and kept him from doing so. Susan then said that she would give us some alone-time and meet us down at the beach later. Joey almost immediately began to laugh which in turn made me offer a teary laugh as well. He then pulled his hand off my leg and placed it around me, then gently kissed me. I was immediately out of my living hell and in my heaven once again.

I sat while Joey made us both malted milks and it was then that I saw, in another cubicle, the girls from down at the beach who had informed me that my uneducated beach dweller was the deflowerer of many a young woman. I realized that I would never believe idle girl-talk ever again, while realizing that if my relationship with Joey was to pass the test of time that I may then well wish to be deflowered by him.

These thoughts were still in my mind when Joey returned with our milkshakes and this time sat across from me so we could converse more easily. We spoke for some time and what I learnt was that Joey wished to experience all facets of life and so if opportunities arose, he would always take them and so had had a myriad of odd jobs and experiences in the past.

I asked if many young women had provided him with many opportunities in the past, to which he replied, "I have read in books of the opportunities had by other men, but as yet, have not been so lucky myself, but am working on creating such an opportunity this very minute. We both laughed at our own dialogue, but both knew that this was no laughing matter and one day we would possibly act on it, but not yet.

The girls in the other cubicle again caught my eye and this time I thought that I could see a look of derision in their eyes, but that may well have been a look of envy, of that I was not sure, but either way, I did not care.

We were soon at the beach where Susan was waiting when I took off my outer clothing, revealing a new bikini which I had just purchased. I could see a look of shock on Joey's features as I sat beside him. It was Susan who asked, "Where was your bikini manufactured?" I replied with pride, "This bikini was made in Paris France, and cost me a small fortune." Susan looked me over and then with the biggest of smiles, commented, "I was unaware of any shortages of materials in France."

Joey smiled at his sister's comment which made me realize that the mannequin that displayed the bikini in the store was perhaps not as well endowed as I was, and the bikini may not be suitable for a person such as myself. I quickly put on the top that I used while jogging which caused both Joey and Susan to break into uncontrollable laughter at my expense.

I dated Joey from that moment on and spent as much time with him down the beach as was practical. We would mostly do things that cost a minimum of money and sometimes he would have supper with my parents and me at home as they seemed to approve of him, of sorts.

Chapter 4.
Joey has Parents?

I thought that everything was going fine until one day when I arrived at the beach where I found Joey with an older woman who was attractive beyond belief and who seemed overly familiar with him, and he with her. I stood watching them for a while and then decided that I was not prepared to share Joey with anyone, especially an older woman, no matter how attractive she may be.

I walked over to them and spoke directly with the older woman, who I must admit, did intimidate me a little, "I see that you seem very familiar with my Joey; why is this so? Are you having an affair with him?" The woman looked at Joey after which they both broke into laughter. "

Of late many people had been laughing at me and here it was again. I was waiting until the laughter was under control before I asked, "And what is so humorous?" to which Joey replied, still with a smile on his face, "My dearest Ashleigh, I have been overly familiar with this beautiful woman ever since, and even before she released me from her womb. Ashleigh, meet my mother, Peggy."

They again started laughing which caused me to realize my shortcomings in evaluating even the most obvious of situations, but still caused me to laugh at myself with them. When all the laughter came to an end, Peggy explained to me that I had captured her son's heart, which she said was no easy feat, and then said that I should come over to have dinner with them so that I could be shown off to Joey's father.

I was for the moment without words, after which I enquired, "I thought that Joey and his father were estranged from one another." Peggy instantly replied, "Many years ago Joey's dad told him that if he was old enough to disobey his rules then he was old enough to look after himself. Joey has been looking after himself ever since, but they have always been the best of friends. I was learning more and more about Joey, the beach dweller, who I had thought was alone in the world without family, only to find that all my preconceptions were wrong again.

It was only a week later that I was sitting having a meal with Joey's mum Peggy and dad John and his sister Susan, who were all curious about me and what my aspirations were. I explained that I wished to attend a university which had not looked promising until my parents had hired Joey as my tutor. I explained that my results were improving out of sight and now it looked as if I may achieve my objectives.

My interrogation continued when Joey's father asked, "Ashleigh, what would you like to do after university?" I answered immediately, "Mr. Harper, I would like to teach history and eventually become a history professor if that is at all possible." This caused everyone to wear a smile while I was hoping that I had not said something to cause ridicule to myself again.

John then stood up and soon came back with a book in his hands and placed it in front of me on the table. John, sitting down, said that this was a history book written by an exceptionally good author and it was about how history is always created by politicians and yet they take no notice of the lessons of history in making decisions for the present.

The book was entitled 'History repeats itself.' I flipped over the book to read the back cover only to find a picture of the author, 'Joey Harper'. As soon as I was over the initial shock, I asked Joey if he had sold many copies. Joey seemed embarrassed when answering, "Just enough to make me ineligible for welfare, and just enough to take a pretty girl to the movies now and then, but not much more."

It was Susan who commented, "My father bought Joey a laptop computer for his thirteenth birthday and told him to write something, and not long after, Joey had finished his first book."

I seemed to be living in the twilight zone, as Joey had turned my realities upside down. Before I met Joey, I thought that beach bums had no interest in life other than surfing, while having few aspirations past surfing and meeting girls. Here, sitting beside me, was an uneducated beach dweller who not only read books but had total comprehension and was also a published novelist. Over the last number of months, I had had to accept that my perception of humanity was no longer restricted to the stereotypes which I had previously characterized everyone in.

I thought that there could no longer be anything left that would take my breath away, but that was to change when I asked, "Joey, have you written any other books?" Joey remained silent as Peggy spoke before he could reply, "Joey makes a little money from writing stories for the Mills and Boon romance book company. He has written many short stories for them."

I smiled as I turned to Joey and asked, "Maybe I have read one of your stories. Do you think that you will ever write a love story about you and me?" Joey turned his head towards me and replied, "My stories have always been about you, even before I met you. The person in my stories has always been looking for you, but at the time didn't even know your name."

Peggy spoke as if she were speaking to herself, as well as the others at the table, "Isn't that sweet." It really was sweet and tender and kind and certainly melted any reservations I had in trying to keep Joey at a safe distance.

After the meal and enlightening conversation, Joey drove me home in his mother's car. On the way, I explained that my parents were away for the weekend, which would allow him to stay the night in my bed. If I thought that Joey would jump at the chance then I was mistaken, as he replied to me, "Ashley, you read the romantic Mills and Boon novels, and so you should understand that is what always occurs at the end of a novel."

"A romantic novel starts with the meeting of two young people, who after some time, show their affection by holding hands which after some more time may lead to a kiss and then a more passionate kiss. They then interact more and more over time which may lead to a passionate embrace where a bosom tries to create indents into a lover's chest. Later, as they interact some more, his arm will brush against her bosom accidentally and he will wish to know whether the tender feelings that he had experienced at that moment are also reciprocated by her. In the final chapter, they share a bed, either by getting married or else by shacking up together."

"You, my dear Ashley, must be the type of person who wishes to read the last chapter first. I on the other hand, while longing for the end myself, wish to experience all the chapters in between."

I knew that Joey did not wish to embarrass me, but I was a little embarrassed as I had never been so forward with anyone ever before. When we arrived home, Joey told me that he loved me and then kissed me after which I left him to go inside.

It was not much later when I was in bed asleep that I heard the window to my bedroom opening. I sat up only to find Joey coming through the window, which amazed me as we lived in a two-story house and my bedroom was on the upper floor. I cannot even remember taking off my clothes but felt Joey's naked body pushing against mine. All my recent dreams were coming to fruition until the ultimate moment passed and I woke up and realized that I had been dreaming.

I should have been disappointed, but strangely was not, as I realized as Joey had said, that there would be many chapters in between, before the final chapter should be experienced, to build up anticipation before a final chapter was even to be considered.

Time went on and I would always chat to Joey in his sleeping bag every morning. Unless there was a bad weather forecast, Joey would always rent out his own room and sleep on the beach. I believed that this was so he could chat with me every morning but of this I was not sure. I was often cold when it was windy as I jogged along, and I believe that this was the reason that I came down with a cold which was soon diagnosed as pneumonia. I was taken to hospital where I thought that I would have to forgo my chats with Joey but that was not to be. I hoped that Joey would visit me but that I thought was not likely. I spent two days in a hospital bed reading my books to keep busy while sleeping in between.

The hospital went through three eight-hour shifts of nurses every day. and so it was that the same nurse would be on duty for the same hours. Mostly, the night nurses seemed like a blur as I was asleep or at least trying to sleep. Most nurses were female with the occasional male nurse in between.

One night, at midnight, I felt a hand in mine lifting my arm to do what I thought must be a blood pressure test. I had been dreaming of Joey, which was not uncommon for me, and in my delirium, I moved what I thought was Joey's hand onto my bosom. I immediately realized what I had done and that the hand was that of a male nurse. I was afraid to open my eyes but was fully awake under the closed eyes.

I tried to move the unwanted hand away from my person only to find that this nurse then kissed me tenderly on my lips. I was perhaps more than a little frightened and so I attempted to sit up as I opened my eyes.

In the darkness I thought that I could see the silhouette of Joey in nurse's uniform. Was I delirious? Did Joey take on the persona of a nurse just to see me? What would happen if he were caught? I was soon awake enough to ask, "Joey what the hell are you doing here?" but the male nurse was gone.

I looked into the semi-darkness trying to make sense of what had just happened. Did a male nurse take advantage of my dream state? Should I report this incident to the doctor on his rounds the following day? I eventually went back to sleep, awakening the following morning to a female nurse who I quizzed about the night nurse. I explained that I thought that the previous night nurse had taken advantage of my drug induced situation and that he had fondled me and kissed me.

I explained that in my dreamlike state, I had pulled his hand onto my bosom which he did not resist, after which he kissed me gently on my lips. Instead of showing any compassion for my situation the nurse replied with, "If I could only be so lucky. I have fancied the night nurse for some time now, but he has some girl who he meets on the beach early every morning who has his complete attention and the female nurses here don't stand a chance."

I had no more to say other than, "Is this male nurse working again tonight?" to which she replied, "Yes, Joey had the night shift again tonight."

Joey? This was too much of a coincidence. This could only be my Joey but what was he doing impersonating a male nurse. I could hardly wait until nightfall when I would try to keep awake so that I could question this male nurse. I didn't want to sleep until I again experienced this male nurse, only to find that it was indeed my Joey. I asked, "Joey, what the hell are you doing here?" Joey replied, "I put myself down to do the night shift soon after I found out that you were admitted." The pills that I was on then took over and I succumbed to sleep almost immediately only to be awaken again for another blood pressure test which was administered by Joey. I was even more confused by being fully awake and asked Joey what he was doing. Joey replied, I moonlight as a nurse, and occasionally when it suits me, I put my name on the list, applying to do night shifts.

Of course, I explained that he needed qualifications to be a nurse to which he replied that he had sat all the nursing exams and passed them all. Joey, then with jovial pride, said that he excelled at bedpan emptying which was in great demand during the night shift.

I was again living in the twilight zone with Joey being a beach dwelling registered nurse. What else was there to my Joey that I did not already know? I was in a daze the following day, waiting for the night when Joey would have to attend to me again when my blood pressure tests were again due. I then explained that I felt an irregular heart rhythm and pulled Joey's hand and placed it on my bosom for him to evaluate. Joey smiled as he told me to behave, otherwise he would request a female nurse to attend to me.

I was released from hospital soon afterwards and started jogging again, finding Joey in his sleeping bag. I quizzed Joey about this occupation to which he replied that he only placed his name on the list when he needed some extra money or when a beautiful girl needed to be looked after.

How complicated a life could a beach dwelling boy have? Once again, Joey had manipulated the system for his own benefit and had received his nurse's qualifications by obviously dubious means to expand his horizons and provide himself with extra money if required.

Time again moved on and we spent the next few weeks experiencing the beginning of the chapters in between when another end term was approaching. Joey was still coming around twice a week as my tutor for free, even though he had completed his task by showing me how to fully comprehend what I was reading. Joey would always be waiting when I arrived home from school. I would normally change out of my school uniform into my jogging outfit as soon as I came home, except for when Joey was there, and I would then wait until after he left.

I was so used to having Joey in my room that one day without even thinking, as Joey immediately began flicking through pages of my textbooks where I had been studying that week, I changed out of my school clothes into my jogging outfit while he was there. Joey's eyes looked up from my book, seeing me in bra and panties putting on my jogging outfit. Joey's eyes then returned to my textbook, and nothing was said.

I may have started on this action before realizing that he was still in my room, but certainly not before I could have stopped. I found that I was acting as the seductress to a reluctant paramour, just as in the books that I read, and I must say that I enjoyed the feeling immensely.

My end term test was this Thursday, and it would be Monday morning when my results would be known. I waited in anticipation, mostly as I wished to please Joey, even more than my ambitions of attaining university status. The Thursday after the test, I came home again to find Joey waiting for me. We made ourselves a cool drink in the kitchen as Joey was enquiring as to how I went in my test. I explained that I was confident but would have to wait until Monday for the results to be known.

As usual, Joey followed me up to my room for the now usual ritual where I would change into my jogging outfit with Joey in the room. What I had not accounted for was that father had arrived home to find my bedroom door open with me still in bra and panties changing into my jogging outfit. Father immediately saw red as he viewed Joey reading my textbook, with me there with my joggers travelling up over my panties to give me some modesty.

Father then asked, "Ashleigh, what in the world are you doing?" I answered as nonchalantly as possible, "I am only changing into my joggers." Father, who was getting more agitated by the moment replied, "Oh, I thought that I was looking at my reserved daughter turning herself into a tramp."

Again, trying to be nonchalant, I replied, "Wearing bra and panties is no more revealing than wearing my bikini down at the beach." Father's voice was raised when he asked Joey, "Do you care to explain the difference to my daughter Ashleigh, or is that above your level of expertise?"

Joey raised his eyes from the book and spoke to my father as if he was just having a normal conversation, "I am only too well aware of the difference Mr. Jackson." Joey then gazed at me and began as if he was a tutor in such matters as well, "Ashleigh, wearing a bikini down the beach, is a fashion statement that states that you are a modern woman and want the world to see you that way, while any state of undress in a bedroom with a guest of the opposite species present, dictates that she is busy with the seduction process of the other person in the room." I was embarrassed beyond belief when father smiled at Joey and spoke appraisingly to him, "Son you seem to know more about life than most people, but if Ashley wishes to get changed in future, you will be standing in the hallway waiting for her to finish with the door shut. Do you understand?"

I was upset with Joey but realized that Joey had diffused a dire situation that could have had catastrophic consequences but was now over with, and it would be business as usual, even though, I still planned to change into my joggers in front of Joey, but only after checking that father's car was not in the drive.

All my expectations were met on Monday when I read on the noticeboard that I had achieved two A+'s plus one A and the remainder were B's. I expected that we would celebrate again but this time I wished to invite Joey's parents as well, as it was his success as well as mine, but first I would like to take in a movie alone with Joey. As yet, Joey had kissed me at different times but certainly not the passionate overpowering kiss that I had read about and seen in the movies which I wanted to experience myself. Joey always let me select the movie and this time I would pay attention to the classification.

The movie was a light romantic comedy which suited me after the embarrassing R rated movie that I had selected the first time. I again put the arm rest down so as I could slide myself under Joey's arm. We shared a popcorn packet and every time I handled the container to take some for myself, I placed the container in a holder on the left side of me while Joey sat on my right, so that Joey would have to reach around me, and his arm would have to brush against my bosom to retrieve it.

I could not believe how it was possible for Joey to reach around me without brushing up against my bosom, but he seemed to be able to do so without any effort at all. Joey seemed so engrossed in the movie that he was unaware of any untoward effort on my part. After my popcorn debacle, I put my arm around Joey as his arm tightened around me.

Every now and then, Joey would gently kiss me on the side of my face near my ear until I turned my head so that his aim was forced to improve, and who then kissed me on my lips. Joey lingered in the position that I placed him in, which was my only real accomplishment that night, but there were to be many more chapters in our book, and I was prepared to savor each and every one.

With the help of Susan, I had arranged my own celebration and soon we were at a fancy restaurant with both families attending. Everyone congratulated me, and to that I replied that my success was mainly due to being tutored by Joey. Joey seemed embarrassed by my assertions, but his parents and my parents were beaming with delight. Joey's father then raised his voice and with a raised volume and a smile, stated, "Joey, just think of how much you could have accomplished if you would have continued on to grade eight." Joey then replied, "I could have accomplished many years of repetitive boredom going over the same thing, over and over again."

Everyone smiled as they thought his statement to be humorous, but I knew better, as I was beginning to know Joey as well as I knew myself, even though I was starting to realize that I did not know myself very well at all. I travelled home with my parents, which was perhaps a little disappointing as I had wanted to push the boundaries of my relationship with Joey, but that would have to wait.

The previous time when we had celebrated my improved scholastic results, I had a dream whereby Joey had magically climbed up the side of our house and come through my window. I laughed at myself when I opened my window, perhaps hoping that such a thing would at all be possible. I lay in bed looking at the window smiling at my ridiculous thoughts until such time that Joey again came through my window and again lay in my bed. We behaved in a similar fashion to my previous dream until such time that I opened my eyes to find that I was dreaming again. If Joey was in reality, half the lover that he was in my dreams, then I would certainly be a happy girl in the final chapter of our book.

I was beginning to believe that my hopes and aspirations of being in a more intimate relationship with Joey would never come to fruition, but I was in fact enjoying the fact that I was participating in writing every line in the story of Joey and Ashleigh. Joey was perhaps correct in his view that there is a journey to be had before the final chapter in any love affair. I was, however, having concerns that there would never be a last chapter at the rate we were progressing.

Chapter 5.
A Failed Seduction.

It was another Thursday when Joey was waiting for me to arrive home, after which as per our usual routine, I was standing in bra and panties in the process of changing into my jogging shorts with my back to Joey. I was a little annoyed at him, as I knew that not another person in all of male humanity would pass up on the chance to at least embrace a young woman standing flaunting herself in her unmentionables. While these thoughts were overtaking my conscious thought, I felt two powerful arms from behind wrap themselves around my upper torso travelling in an upward direction. They moved upwards until their path was restricted by my bosom.

I felt Joey's lips apply pressure between my shoulder and my neck which made me realize that our story had not become as stagnant as I had thought but was moving along at a pace that I had no way of quickening. Before I realized what or how, Joey had lifted me off the ground and had placed me on my bed and lay himself beside me. We kissed and cuddled in an intimate fashion with Joey's hands on my lower cheeks pulling me to him. I had never been in so intimate a situation ever before, and I should have restricted myself, but did no such thing.

I could have been content by laying in Joey's arms forever, but it was not to be as I could hear mother's car pulling into our driveway. I pushed my lips onto Joey's for one last time before rushing to finish putting on my jogging outfit. Both Joey and I were in position when mother came up the stairs to announce that she was home and to greet us.

Mother asked me how I was and received my reply that I was well. She then asked Joey the same while looking at the rumpled state of my bed. Joey, realizing the situation, replied with a smile, "Your daughter tried to molest me, and I had to fight her off. If this type of behavior continues, then I will have to withdraw my services as her tutor." I was shocked. I was horrified. How could Joey say such a thing, especially to my mother. My very existence was threatened, but mother only smiled at Joey and said, "Being a tutor to an adolescent girl has many pitfalls, but I am sure that you will prevail. I will make both of you a cup of tea as it can be relaxing and is also known to cool a person's libido."

I could not believe that my mother could speak to Joey in such a fashion and treat our obvious attempts at intimacy as acceptable behavior. I also began to realize that Joey could not only fully comprehend what was written in books but could read my mother better than I could read her myself. I decided that I had learnt a valuable lesson and if the same situation happened again, I would first make sure to straiten my bed. Mother left the room which made Joey break into laughter, but this was no laughing matter for me, as my mother would never see me as her prim and proper, reserved daughter, ever again.

That night as I lay in my bed, I realized how my life had changed from when I saw a sleeping bag perched in the soft sand on the beach with who I considered was an uneducated beach dweller inside, whose mental aspirations went no further than hoping for a decent wave to appear on the horizon. This handsome boy had changed my very being, and yet I seemed to categorize him only slightly differently now than previously, even though he occupied the top position in my heart.

At school that day, I was again summoned to the principal's office and was again told to sit on the chair on the other side of his desk, which was a privilege, as most students were forced to stand. As soon as I sat down, principal Ben Jacobs began to speak, "Ashleigh, I know that you are not cheating, but am forced to investigate such changes in a student's state of end term results. The only explanation that you have provided me, is that you have a tutor of about your age who even though only attaining the primary year seven education has the intellect and capabilities to not only improve you but change you into a grade A student who is competing with the other grade A students in her class."

"I have looked through our old school records and even though Joey Harper excelled in year seven, he cannot have progressed further from there and must still be a relatively illiterate boy without having attended any learning institution."

I was incensed that he called my Joey illiterate, and so I replied, "Joey is not illiterate, as he is the author of a published novel." There was a moment of silence after which Ben continued speaking, "And what is the title of this so-called novel?" I proudly replied, "The novel is called, 'History repeats itself'."

Not only was there silence, but this time Ben's mouth was ajar while his eyes stared through me. Ben stood and walked over to his bookshelf and pulled out Joey's book. Ben began speaking even before sitting down, "I have read this book more than once and this book was definitely not written by an eighteen-year-old boy." I smiled as I replied, "You are indeed correct Sir, as Joey was only thirteen at the time of writing."

Mr. Jacobs then frantically turned over the book to find a reference to the author, only to be staring into a small picture of thirteen-year-old Joey with his name beside the picture. Ben spoke as though he was speaking to himself as well as me, "I had thoughts that the writer of this book must have been an older person, at least in his late fifties or older. The reference information which is contained in this book could only have been attained by years of reading and evaluation."

I sat waiting in silence while Ben stared at his desk for what seemed an eternity, then quietly began, "I have heard of such child prodigies but have never met one in my entire life. I would like to meet with him so that I can send in my report to say that there is no cheating going on." Ben then explained that educational computers take note of massive changes to students results throughout the state to eliminate cheating, and whenever a red flag comes up, it must be investigated.

Ben then asked, "Could you please arrange for Joey and yourself to come in one afternoon at three thirty after school hours so that we can put this matter behind us. I agreed, as I had Joey on Thursday afternoons to myself anyway, and so knew that he would not be committed elsewhere.

Thursday afternoon came, and soon Joey and I were sitting in two chairs in front of my principal, Ben Jacobs. Ben then asked, "Joey, do you realize that I am forced to investigate Ashleigh's scholastic improvements, in order to fill in a report to state that she has not been cheating by achieving such end term improvements?

I could see that Joey was enjoying his reply, "Ben, if I may call you by your Christian name, Ashleigh's results were attained solely by Ashleigh and only Ashleigh. I only provided a love for reading and comprehension and a retention of that knowledge."

Ben smiled as if he was playing a game of cat and mouse, "Maybe you could show me how to get a student to retain more of what he or she has read, as that has always been my ambition also." Joey looked every part a teacher as he was replying to the principle's request, "Ben, I believe that mankind has three types of memory, a long-term memory, a short-term memory and a short-short-term memory. Have you ever stood up in your chair to get an item only to find that you have immediately forgotten why you stood up in the first place?"

"When most people dream, they retain their dream in their short-short-term memory which is mostly unable to be recalled as soon as one is awake, but if, let us say for a moment, it is a male who is having a dream about an appealing female who is not too concerned about retaining all of her clothing on her shapely body, then this male upon waking may have full recall of everything from the clothing which she discarded, to the degree of curvature of her anatomy, to the bounce of her hair, to the smell of her perfume."

Ben then also smiled, "You, of course, are telling me what all of male humanity is well aware of." Joey then ignored this interruption and then continued, "Why then can he have vivid recollections of these dreams compared to other dreams? It is because a basic human being wishes to know everything about the opposite of his own species, instilled in him by the mating requirements of all creatures, and so, his mind has placed this detailed knowledge into his long-term memory to recall later. If one could create such a mindset in a person who wishes to recall every intricate detail of everything that is read or experienced, then would not that bypass his short-term memory and pass into his long-term memory to be recalled when required?"

"I have taught Ashleigh to savor every piece of information in every chapter in her books. Ashleigh has replaced her body's search for knowledge about intimacy with the search of all knowledge. Incentive also plays a major part in the will for retention of relevant knowledge. Ashleigh thinks that I will sleep with her if her results improve out of sight, and I believe that this incentive has made her embrace every piece of knowledge found in any of these books."

I had been embarrassed many times of late, but never had I been embarrassed to such an extent in my entire life. How could Joey make such a statement, even though it was possibly true? Did he really believe that my wanting to spend some intimate time with him had driven me on to my scholastic achievements, and was he using this fact as a tool to help me, and if so, did he return my feelings for him? And how in God's creation did Joey think that he could talk of this so openly with my principal?

These thoughts immediately pounded my brain as their conversation had paused, after which Mr. Jacobs asked, "Ashleigh, is it your desire to sleep with Joey and if so, did this help in your ability to retain the knowledge found in your books?"

It took me a moment to form my reply so as to keep some of my dignity, "Every girl during her puberty years and beyond, dreams about intimacy with a desirable boy and I do not believe that I am any different, but whether a girl acts on such feelings is not necessarily a certainty, and as for if it has helped me in my scholastic ability, I could not say." I was proud of myself with such a reply as this had been a precarious situation where I could have easily lost much of my standing in his eyes.

Ben then laughingly replied to Joey, "I believe that the parents of my feminine students would immediately demand my removal if I made such promises to their daughters, and I am sure that my wife would be non to thrilled with the idea as well."

Ben and Joey laughingly continued their conversation as if nothing untoward had happened, until Joey said that he had to take me home, after which we left.

On the way home I berated Joey about how the conversation with my principal had progressed, in that I wished to be intimate with him. Joey only laughed at me which infuriated me even more, until he said, "It is natural for any young person to desire another, and to hope that those feelings are reciprocated. The first moment that I saw you when I was sleeping on the beach and opened my eyes, I already wanted to pull you into my sleeping bag with me, but while looking into your eyes, I could not see any reciprocated feelings and so I went back to sleep."

While walking home, I placed my hand into Joey's, and after some thought, asked, "And so Joey, when did you say that you would be sleeping on the beach again?" Joey laughed as if I was joking but I kept a stern look on my features to show that this was no laughing matter.

My scholastic achievements were now as such that Joey was no longer tutoring me but instead was dating me. We would often see movies; go to parties; meet down at the beach and to my complete satisfaction often kissed and cuddled laying in the sand in our swimmers. This was always the highlight to what I considered was my very being, but of course, being a maturing girl, I wanted more.

I thought that Joey was playing the part of the reluctant female that I had always read about in my Mills and Boon novels which meant that I would have to play the part of the aggressive male in a complete role reversal to what humanity expected. I always remembered what Joey had told me, in that I wished to read the last chapter before experiencing all the chapters in between. I enjoyed all the chapters in between but of course could not wait until the story's ultimate and intimate conclusion.

Life went on and my end term results just got better each term. Joey would often come over to my house where we would read books. Joey, however, read about five to ten books by the time I had read one. While my reading was slowed by feeling him squeezed beside me on my bed, I seemed to have little effect on him. Having Joey lying beside me reading in my bed was now accepted by my parents, even though I still felt uncomfortable when my parents would venture into my room under some pretext in order to keep an eye on us.

It was a weekend when I was lying on my bed, once again in my undergarments, with my parents visiting some friends of theirs, that the door to my room opened without any knocking beforehand. I stared into the face of Joey who eyed me for only a moment and then took off his own clothes down to his boxer shorts and lay beside me, embracing me with his tanned hairless chest pushed against my exposed brassiere. I was certainly not expecting this and almost shook with anticipation when he kissed me and said that he was going to make my dreams come true. I held Joey even tighter until he said that my favorite Mills and Boon novel had been made into a movie and that he had purchased tickets for us both to see it that very afternoon.

I was elated but still disappointed as that was not my number one choice of possible outcomes to all my expectations. I rolled on top of Joey and decided that I would give my all in trying to move forward to our last chapter, but to no avail as Joey pushed me off him and told me that we were still in the middle of our novel. I could, however, feel that his mind controlled his actions as I felt that his body had wished to proceed with the matter at hand before he pushed me off him.

Joey and I were soon at the picture theatre viewing my favorite Mills and Boon story with Joey's arms around me. The reason that this story was my favorite was that the female character was the aggressor, and the male played the reluctant romantic, even though he was hopelessly in love with the pretty young girl from their very first meeting. I perhaps related this story to Joey and myself which may have been the reason that it was my favorite.

I knew the story was authored by Wendy Marshal whose stories I loved. I would always choose her stories over all others and had read all her work and felt as if I knew her. I knew that Wendy was only slightly older than I was, as I had read her author's description many times. I was appalled when driving home and Joey stated that it was he who had authored the novel.

I immediately became incensed at Joey's claim as to being the author, as I knew for a fact that Wendy Marshal had been responsible for the story. Joey went on to explain that often, females relate to other females when reading such novels, and so many of his stories are written under the penname of Wendy Marshal. I sat in shock trying to comprehend how all my prior conceptions had been false, in that my favorite novelist was a male, and not only that, but was my Joey.

After my immediate shock had subsided, Joey smiled as he asked, "Tell me Ashleigh, how does it feel, by participating in a lesbian relationship with Wendy Marshal?" I gave Joey a stern look and a sarcastic reply, "My relationship with you has not progressed any further that it would have if you were a female, and so I believe that you are well qualified in portraying Wendy Marshal."

I did not mean for my statement to be humorous, but it did cause Joey to break into laughter, to my consternation. When we arrived home, I was still upset, while finding my parents still not at home. I made some cool drinks for Joey and me and went up to my bedroom, where, as usual, I would change into my comfortable day clothes. At first, I had changed in front of Joey to be seductive or perhaps sensually teasing, but now it was just commonplace. I discarded my outer clothes leaving me in bra and knickers only to find that Joey stood in his boxer shorts with his arms around me.

Joey then spun me around and pulled me to him and kissed me. He then explained that it was time for our relationship to progress to the next level. Joey pushed me away from himself sufficiently enough to place his hands on the clip which held my brassiere together from the front. Instead of viewing and fondling what was now on offer to him, he released my bosom from its enclosure and pulled me to him so that my bosom pushed hard into his tanned hairless chest. I was wondering if this would be the last chapter in the romantic tale of Ashleigh and Joey, but after some time cuddling on my bed and not progressing any further, I realized that there were perhaps more similar chapters to be had before our ultimate chapter.

Was I material for another of the stories that he would be sending to Mills and Boon? Was he playing some perverse game with me, or was he giving me appreciation by anticipating what was to happen in our final chapter? I did not know, but what I did know was that I was enjoying every moment of my own crazy love story and wanted to read on.

Time moved on and I was now halfway through my senior year when my eighteenth birthday was approaching. My parents planned a birthday party for me and my friends, after which, on Joey's prompting, I told my parents that a few of us wanted to spend time at the beach talking around a small fire until morning, so that we could watch the sunrise.

I had never expected my parents to agree, but they gave me permission to do so, as long as I was in the company of Joey. I would have thought that Joey would have been their greatest deterrent in allowing me to do so, but that did not seem to be the case. My party was held at a local restaurant, after which a few of the diehards went down to the beach with Joey and me where we lit a fire and talked well into the morning.

We all sat talking beside the fire when we were approached by two police officers who informed us to douse the fire before we left and place the unburnt timber into the shrubbery above the sand. One of the officers then recognized Joey and then stated, "Joey, you know how it is done. Where is your container for the water? Joey then pointed to his collapsible water container and then the policemen bid us a good night.

Eventually, one by one, the party diehards offered their excuses, saying that they were tired and were going home and to bed. This left Joey and me to walk hand in hand on the hard sand until we came to the exact spot where I had at first spotted a homeless, ill-educated boy sleeping on the upper beach. I placed my arm around Joey and asked if he remembered this exact spot.

Joey never answered but said that he wanted to live a fantasy that had plagued his dreams ever since we had met, which now seemed such a long time ago. Joey walked up the beach, high into the shrubbery behind the dune and came back with a plastic bag in which were his sleeping bag and a ground sheet. Joey placed the ground sheet on the soft sand on which he placed his sleeping bag. Joey then stripped down to his boxer shorts and slipped into the sleeping bag. I was confused by what was happening but then Joey told me to stand in the same position that I had on the day that I had first met him.

Chapter 6.
Ashley the woman.

I realized that we were playing a mind game, **his** mind game, and so did as I was asked. Joey feigned sleep as I bent over him as he opened his eyes and muttered, "Good morning." I replied with, "Good morning", but now instead of again closing his eyes when we first met, Joey asked, "Would you care to keep me company in my sleeping bag, and if so, take off your outer coverings and brush the sand off your feet beforehand?"

I liked playing games, especially this type of game and so I soon lay beside Joey in his sleeping bag. I had waited for this moment for over a year and a half and planned to savor every moment. When I entered Joey's sleeping bag, I would be an eighteen-year-old girl, but I knew that when I awoke in the morning and removed myself from his sleeping bag, I would be an eighteen-year-old woman.

There was a cool breeze when I awoke with Joey's head resting just above my bosom under my chin with his arm draped over me. I was in heaven, as I had dreamt of this very moment, countless times, but was never sure that it would ever happen to me. Soon we were both sitting up in our sleeping bag looking at the light on the horizon which meant that the sun was trying to rise to warm us up.

Without thinking, I said to Joey that one day I would like to have a baby. If Joey was not fully awake, he soon was, and began to berate me, "God almighty girl, last night we have just completed the final chapter of our own Mills and Boon novel, and you are wanting to move to the end chapter of, not only book two, but book three. We are just about to commence on book two, and I have a proposition to put to you, now that you are a complete woman."

It sounded good to be called a woman and I needed to feed my womanly curiosity and ask what his proposition was. Joey began, "Soon you will have completed your senior year and will be ready for university, whereas, I will have to wait for another two years until I qualify under the adult education program. With your approval, I suggest that you take a two-year gap period so that you can go on a working holiday with me around the country and perhaps even overseas and then begin university together, after which we will then be able to share accommodation costs at university."

This was a lot for me to take in and I would have to give it my consideration. I knew that I wished to pursue a career in historical studies but was still not aware as to what Joey's plans were, and so I asked him. Joey replied, "I plan to obtain a degree in Electrical Engineering, a degree in Chemical engineering and a diploma in applied mathematics." I was perhaps not surprised but still asked, "And you plan to do these all at the same time do you?"

Joey replied with, "Yes, that is the plan, and is not unheard of, as quite a few people have accomplished that very thing in the past." I had no doubt that Joey could accomplish such a feat, and as I had given myself to him, I would not so easily let him get away from me. I had to give his proposition more thought but had already realized that I would do exactly as he suggested.

I asked what type of jobs we would pursue, and Joey as usual, had planned ahead. Joey explained, "While working on the fishing trawler, Annabelle, I sat for various skipper-licenses and obtained them all. I have an opportunity to skipper a luxury craft early next year for some rich guy and can select my own mate. I believe I may have selected my own mate last night." Joey received a coy smile from me after which I explained that the sun had not yet risen above the horizon, and we should slide down into his sleeping bag to keep warm.

Joey was no fool and had long ago realized that what a woman says and what she means are not necessarily the same, and so we were again in his sleeping bag satisfying another purpose altogether than just keeping warm. It was that morning when I walked along the beach with Joey, that my life seemed to have changed. Joey rested his arm on my shoulder as we walked along the beach to the milk bar for our free breakfast. I knew that I had found my partner in life, even though we were both still in our teenage years.

I was apprehensive about going home and telling my parents about my plans, In that I would take two gap years to work and travel with Joey before starting university. The milk bar was still not open and so Joey and I ended up going home to have breakfast with my parents. While having breakfast with mom and dad, I explained to them of my plans to take two gap years travelling with Joey, before attending university.

I had thought that World War Three would have broken out, but instead, after a prolonged silence, mother replied, "At eighteen, you are now what is considered a woman by law and we cannot force you to do our will anyway, and so the opinions of your parents are of no consequence. Thanks to Joey and your own hard work, you at least have a chance at attending university and so your future looks more promising than it did two years ago."

I could hardly believe how well that had gone but could see that mother wished to talk to me privately. After breakfast, Joey went to his own home, and I went to sleep. It was two o'clock in the afternoon when mum brought me a cup of tea and sat beside me on my bed. Mother began on what was a mother daughter talk, "Ashleigh, as you seem to be intimate with

Joey and have future events planned, a woman has to be careful not to let anything untoward happen to her." I knew what she was getting at and so I replied, "Joey and I are careful and use protection."

I could not believe that I was having such a conversation with my mother as if she were only an acquaintance of mine, perhaps a girlfriend who would share intimate details with me, and I her. Had my mother disappeared and who was this woman who I was talking to? I looked at my mother who I knew now saw me in a different light.

Mum just looked at me and said, "I didn't mean that, I mean that men and women at such a young age are constantly changing, and that Joey or yourself may one day decide to move on, and so you should plan your future with that possibility in mind." I was shocked, as I had never even considered it a possibility, but knew in the back of my mind that this was part and parcel of the humanity that I was part of.

Mother's eyes then looked at the floor as she continued talking, "When I was your age, I gave my heart and soul to a young man about Joey's age who eventually moved on to another girl who he found physically more appealing than me, with a humongous bosom that I could never compete with." Mother initially looked sad but then laughed, "And now it is not only her bosom which is humongous but the rest of her as well." Mother then explained that at my age, the future is never certain, and if things do not go as per my expectation with Joey, who they loved as well, then there will be more opportunities available. Mother then continued to my original assumption, in that I was careful and used protection against pregnancy.

Talking to mother had been different to ever before, as we spoke more as woman to woman rather than mother and daughter. I considered that my first choice of a boy in my life would not necessarily have to follow the same path as my mother's initial choice. I thanked her for her motherly advice but immediately discarded these thoughts, even though they would remain in the recesses of my brain. I had already, mistakenly, contemplated those possibilities with Susan, Annabelle, and Joey's own mother, as being possible love interests of his, but would be more careful in future.

It seemed as if I had the perfect existence; a handsome intelligent boyfriend; good grades to allow me to enter university to pursue my chosen profession, and a chance to travel with someone who would be a companion and keep me warm at night. I did, however, realize that I was not yet there, and had to continue studying to the last possible moment to make this all possible. Joey and my parents had complete confidence in me which was a complete turnaround from almost two years previously, when my parents thought that good grades and university acceptance were beyond me.

I returned to my study program with Joey doing his best to help me but was now somewhat of a distraction. Previously I had wanted Joey as a girl does a boy who seems out of her reality, but I now knew that Joey was available to me. Joey, however, seldom acted in any other way than my tutor while in my room to my complete displeasure even though I knew that it was for the best. My matriculation exams were coming up and I displayed nervous confidence waiting until that final day.

I endured one full week of exams after which I would wait until our results were placed in the state newspapers. This was an excruciating time but there was no more study to be done while I waited to find if I had a future or not. After my exams, I was constantly with Joey, either down the beach or seeing movies or going to end of year parties.

Chapter 7.
My competion.

My friends had thought that I would dump Joey now that I was admitted to university, as they still saw him as the illiterate but likeable beach dwelling beach-bum. They still had the impression of Joey as the beach dweller and deflowerer of virgins and thought that I was using him for my immediate enjoyment and no more. When I told them that I was taking two gap years so that Joey and I could travel, after which we would go to university together, they seemed stunned beyond all reason. I explained to them that Joey was extremely intelligent and was planning to attend university under the adult education program when he was twenty-one years of age. I explained that Joey was also a published novelist and our principal had one of his books in his office library.

Mostly, I received only blank stares with mouths slightly ajar, which I must admit that I enjoyed. People had previously often talked down to Joey which had annoyed me, even though Joey seemed to thrive, in that people thought of him as being stupid.

I had created a nightmare for myself, as all the girls now wanted to chat with Joey who they now saw in a different light. He was no longer the degenerate, illiterate, beach dweller who any respectable girl should stay away from but was now considered well worth chasing after. I saw the possibility of mother's younger-year experience being duplicated by her daughter, but Joey brushed all the would-be seductresses aside and always came back to me, at least that is what I thought until Joey again went missing.

I had the standard thoughts of a teenage girl whose boyfriend was nowhere to be found and thought the worst, in that he may well have found another girl with who to occupy his time. After the initial uncertainty passed, I realized that I had made a fool of myself in the past by assuming the worst and embarrassing myself and would not do so again.

I pulled myself together and tried to proceed in a more logical way. Joey and I had our future planned, so why would he jeopardize this for a weekend away with some other girl. I thought that I would get in contact with Joey's sister Susan as she always knew what Joey was up to and so went directly to find her.

I rang Joey's parents and asked where Susan was and if they knew where Joey was. They replied that they had no idea as to where Joey was, but Susan could probably be found at the beach milk bar. I immediately made my way down to the milk bar only to find her talking to friends. After she saw me, she extradited herself from her friends and came over to me and we grabbed a booth and sat down with coffee, ordered from the waitress.

I immediately asked if she knew where Joey was, to which she replied that he was taking the long weekend away with Katie, camping along with some other girls. I was instantly horrified but noticed the hidden smile of Susan showing through her sullen statement. I had been made a fool of many times of late, mainly caused by my own mistaken presumptions and now was wary to jump to such erroneous conclusions so quickly again.

I quickly realized that Susan was enjoying my confusion but still asked, "And why would Joey go off on a weekend camping with whoever Katie is and with a bunch of other girls?" Susan replied, "Joey has known Katie for nearly four long years now, and if Katie tells Joey to jump, Joey only asks, 'How high'?"

I was shaken but still realized that Susan was trying to take the mickey out of me but still asked, "And how did Joey come to meet Katie?" Susan smiled as she replied, "Joey was sleeping on the beach over four years ago, when after midnight, Katie woke him up by tripping over his sleeping bag. After realizing that it was a person in a sleeping bag, Katie explained that she was freezingly cold and stood visibly shaking. Joey, realizing the severity of the situation, told Katie to hop into the sleeping bag with him to keep warm, which she did until the sun rose and warmed them both. Joey then took care of Katie as best he could by feeding her breakfast, and now if Katie asked something of Joey, then Joey always complies to her wishes."

Susan was just like her brother Joey in that she never lied, but sometimes could be purposely misleading and so I was again beginning to feel insecure in my relationship with Joey. I wanted to confront the situation as to where I stood in Joey's affection compared to Katie, and so I asked if Susan was prepared to take me to Joey where he was camping. Susan readily agreed and off we went in her car.

It was 8 PM in the evening when we arrived, well after dark. Susan parked the car and we had to walk to where they were camping. As we approached the site, I could see a fire surrounded by young girls of about twelve years of age including Joey and a Catholic nun who was partly in habit over a pair of jeans and boots. I was confused again when getting closer to this unlikely group of campers. They all had sticks and on the end of the sticks were marshmallows which they were warming over the fire and then putting into their mouths.

They were all shocked as Susan and I appeared out of the darkness. After the shock was absorbed by everyone, Joey motioned for us to sit, as he had just placed a complete marshmallow in his mouth. When the marshmallow was fully in his stomach, Joey asked, "What are you two doing here?" I replied, "I have come to meet my competition, Katie." The young girl who was sitting beside Joey then spoke up, "I am Katie, you must be Ashleigh."

Being with Joey was always like living in the twilight zone and now was no different. Seeing that I was confused, Susan with the help of the woman in nun's habit explained away my confusion.

Susan began, "Young Katie was seven when her parents were killed in a traffic accident after which she was placed in an orphanage run by the catholic nuns. Katie was barely eight when she ran away from the orphanage and began living on the streets, and that was when one night she wandered down to the beach with a breeze blowing, upon which time she began to shake and shiver. Katie then tripped over Joey's sleeping bag on the beach, waking him up and explaining to him that she was freezing. Joey then took her into his sleeping bag with him until the morning sun warmed up the world around them. When they both had breakfast at the milk bar, Katie explained her situation to him, in that she had run away from the orphanage and was now homeless. Katie explained that the orphanage was okay but wanted to be part of a family, just as before with her parents."

"Joey realized that he was street wise and a boy, and that the streets were no place for an innocent girl like little Katie. Joey was aware that there was an immigrant German family who were seeking to adopt a little girl, as the lady was unable to bare children herself. The hopeful parents had been rejected by the adoption agency as their grip on the English language was as yet inadequate to meet stipulated requirements."

"The family had just arrived from Germany and so they would need some time to learn to speak fluid English which of course would come over time. Joey was aware of Sister Luke who was, in reality Mother Superior at the orphanage, and went to see her if an underhanded deal could be done to unite Katie with the young German couple."

"Sister Luke was only too happy to get Katie off the streets and so forged some paperwork to allow Katie into a loving family. The couple, Kurt and Helga, were over the moon and were grateful to Joey and often invited him over to lunch to spend time with them and Katie."

"From that moment on, if Katie needed Joey, he would instantly comply to her wishes. The usual orphanage male guardian and all-round helper was sick and as Katie wanted to spend time with her orphanage friends, she asked Joey if he could fill in."

I now sat with a marshmallow in my mouth with my mind contemplating just how complex the life of a beach bum could be. My own life, I had previously thought of as complex and had thought that a beach bums' life would have been very limited but now realized the error of my thought process. I placed my arm around Joey, only to feel Katies arm around him from the other side. Katie arched her body around Joey so that she could look at me and then smiled at me.

Before I arrived at the camp site, I was not prepared to share Joey with any other female but now had no objections anymore with Katie. I asked Joey how it was that Katie knew about me to which he replied, "I have no secrets from Katie and tell her everything." I smiled as I asked Katie, "What do you think now that you know that Joey has a girlfriend?" Katie replied, "I think that Joey and you should get married and have many children and then I can be Aunt Katie to them." Joey then broke into the conversation and replied to Katie, "Ashley and I have not even started on that book as yet, but we will keep that in mind."

Sister Luke told all the girls that it was their bedtime after which they all disappeared into their various tents. Susan said that she wanted to go home and did so, which left me with Joey and Sister Luke who conversed well into the night. Eventually the conversation slowed, and we knew that it was time to turn in. I was perhaps embarrassed when it became obvious that I would sleep with Joey in his tent. Sister Luke, as if she had read my mind, informed me not to be embarrassed as she was not always a nun and was aware of the world around her.

I gave her an appreciative smile after which Joey held my hand to help me stand, after which I followed him to his tent. I slid in beside Joey into his sleeping bag and explained that I was cold after which he proceeded to keep me warm during the night. Of course, me being myself, I instigated more than just sleeping before we succumbed to sleep, being careful not to create too much movement in our tent.

There was a storm at some time during the night. I was the first to awaken in the morning only to find that we had company, as in a sleeping bag beside us was Katie who must have entered our tent during the night, bringing her sleeping bag with her. I always felt embarrassed while interacting with Joey and now was no different as I was unsure of just how long Katie had lay beside us and was embarrassed by it.

To my relief, when Katie awoke, she said that she had been afraid of the storm, and only then came into Joey's tent. Sister Luke was already stoking the fire when Katie, Joey and I emerged from the tent. I realized that Sister Luke was no prude when she smiled and spoke to Joey with, "Joey, it must have been heaven to you, waking up with two females keeping you company during the night."

Joey, who was not to be gotten the better of, replied, "My tent has the capacity to hold one more in case you are also frightened by the storm." Sister Luke returned a smile before answering, "Luckily for me, I enjoy listening to storms, which has prevented me from many a cardinal sin in the past."

I could see just how familiar Joey was with Sister Luke and so stayed out of their conversation. I spoke with Katie near the fire, realizing that Katie knew all about Joey and me and was aware that I had just turned eighteen. I again asked Joey how it was that Katie knew all about us, to which he replied, "I have no secrets from Katie and tell her everything." I never thought that I would have to share Joey with another female but was not concerned if his other love interest would be likeable, loveable little Katie.

We, as happy campers, stayed another night, and the following day were picked up by a small bus belonging to the orphanage and driven home. Joey and I were dropped off at the beach where I said goodbye to Joey and proceeded to walk home.

Chapter 8.
The suspect?

Things were again back to normal when I was again jogging along the hard sand of the beach. About a kilometer down the beach, I came across what I thought was about fifty or more policemen gathered and as I came closer, they stopped me and asked me a barrage of questions. They enquired as to if I often jogged along the beach to which I answered in the affirmative. They explained that a girl had been held captive in the shrubbery above the sand for six days and had been beaten to within an inch of her life.

They asked if I had seen anything suspicious or had seen any strange young men frequenting the area. I explained that I had seen nothing unusual and said that they should contact Joey as he knew of most of the goings-on on the beach. Looking back that may have been a mistake, as Joey instantly became a person of interest in their investigation. They asked Joey to come to the police station for a full interview. Joey, being Joey, of course thought that this would be another adventure and was eager to go down to be interviewed. It was soon that Joey was given the third degree as to who he knew was down the beach during this period which began only weeks after we had returned from the camping trip.

Joey gave a list of people who he knew frequented this area along the beach which were mainly surfing buddies of his. Joey suggested that they also be interviewed as they may have noticed something out of the ordinary. Joey also suggested that they view the surveillance tape of the board shop which he knew pointed towards the beach, even though it was some distance away from the store to the beach.

The interviewer gave Joey the third degree and was annoyed in that he seemed to enjoy the interview. After two hours of finding out that Joey practically lived on the beach and sometimes slept not far from where the assault occurred, he was considered their number one suspect until someone better came along. The interview was almost over when a senior police officer walked past the interview room and saw Joey through the one-way mirror.

The head cop, Samuel Johnston, interrupted the interview and asked why they were interviewing Joey Harper. All was explained in that at present he was their number one suspect and had constantly lied to them without even giving them a hint that he was lying. Samuel then asked what lies they caught him on. The interviewer then replied by saying that Joey lied to irrelevant questions but still lied. He said that Joey had said that he had tutored students after school hours and that was just after he admitted to living on the beach since year seven at school and having never gone back to school ever again.

Samuel Johnstone then laughed when he responded, "I know Joey quite well, as he tutored my imbecilic son into becoming an A grade student. I have never noticed Joey ever lying, so do not so easily discard what he says as being anything but truthful.

The police interviewer, John Clarkson, apparently annoyed at this interruption from his superior, told Joey not to leave the vicinity as they may wish to interrogate him further in the future. With Samuel still present, Joey explained that he would be leaving at the end of February to work on a powered yacht in Brisbane Australia and had a six-month contract. Joey then explained that he knew most of the young men who were familiar with the beach environs and could be of help introducing and interviewing suspects.

The police detective, who was obviously annoyed by the brazen statement from who he considered a suspect, explained that they did not work with prime suspects but instead kept a close eye on them. It was then that Samuel suggested that if Joey was permitted to accompany the investigators, then he may well be of help to them, and they would know of his movements which would alleviate the effort of having to keep track of him.

From that moment on, Joey accompanied John and helped him in meeting many people familiar with that region of the beach. From surveillance tapes from many stores, many possible would-be suspects were identified who frequented the area during the five-day period of the abduction and assault. A selection of young men was asked to come down to the police station the following day for informal interviews, which they all agreed to.

Joey was permitted to view the statement of the victim in which the girl said that she was blindfolded with cotton wool over her eyes and tape wrapped around her head. The assailant had frequently tried to molest her but was physically unable to do so. Every time that he failed, the perpetrator would become frustrated and beat her with his fists. There were times when he would tie her to a small tree and go and get them food and drink, after which he would feed her and himself and again begin on the cycle of failed molestations and beatings.

Joey had read enough and accompanied John, which was mainly at the police station. Joey was not permitted into the interview rooms but was allowed to stand on the other side of the one-way mirror when the interviews were in progress. John was in progress with one of the possible suspects when Joey listened in on the conversation. The long-haired young man explained that he had not been on the beach but only went to the beach precinct to buy food and drink. John came out of the interview room to find Joey waiting for him with a request.

Joey asked John to return to the interview and tell the suspect that the next interviewer would be a policewoman and to provide the suspect with a comb and tell him to make himself presentable and comb his hair. John was confused but still adhered to Joey's wishes and then came out of the room and stood watching the young man comb his unruly long hair.

John asked Joey as to what could be achieved by this as they watched the young man struggle with the comb in his knotted hair. Joey explained that if one were to spend many days on the beach, then one's hair would absorb the salt from the wind blowing over the turbulent waves and become knotted. Only by shampooing hair with fresh water would one be able to wash out the salt. Joey then told John to observe the comb which should contain remnants of salt spray.

Joey also explained that the suspects skin displayed salt burn from the wind which was common when spending days on the beach. John stood speechless and then told Joey that the young man had said that he spent no time on the beach at all and so must be lying. John then said he would continue the interview with a more abrasive line of questioning.

That same afternoon, the victim was permitted to evaluate a lineup of voices and she immediately picked out the young man of the interview as being the culprit.

Joey then asked John if he would now be permitted to leave at the end of the month without the fear of being called back for another interview in the future. John, with a huge smile then said that he had more cases that Joey could accompany him with if he had the time. Joey returned the smile and shook John's hand and said that he had no wish to put John out of a job and then departed.

I could not understand why Joey would think that being the suspect in a police enquiry could be adventurous or even appealing. This mystery would not be solved by me for many years but as for now I found it perhaps more than just a little confusing.

Chapter 9.
Our first adventure.

Another adventure was had by Joey, and it would soon be late February when we were to work on the luxury yacht for a rich guy who was a millionaire many times over. Our contract would be for six months from Brisbane Australia, up around New Guinea and surrounds, down the east coast and over to many islands to the east. The last skipper had left the boat anchored near the port of Brisbane awaiting our arrival as well as the arrival of her owner. We were met at the terminal by the owner who picked us up in the boat's tender and ferried us over to where the yacht was anchored.

The man was Robert Denning who seemed a bit passed his prime and who said that he was expecting his teenage daughter, who was a product of his and his estranged wife, to accompany us for as long as she wished to stay. Joey and I could see a look of frustration in his eyes when he spoke of his daughter but said no more. The next day Robert's fifteen-year-old daughter Candy arrived. We picked her up in the yacht's tender and took her to see her father who she seldom saw and was apprehensive as to why her father had insisted that she come along. As soon as the formalities of the meeting were over, we were soon underway northward. Skies were clear, winds were slight, and so we anticipated a smooth voyage.

Candy was a pretty girl who chatted about all the brainless chit-chat that mindless teenage girls often do. This girl seemed to know everything that was happening in Hollywood, down to what color toenail polish, Britney Spears wore that week. Candy's father tried to seem interested by his daughter's ramblings, but even Candy realized that she was out of her depth when trying to hold an intelligent conversation with her own father. The afternoon passed with Candy lying on the rear deck while sunning herself and listening to the radio in her little bikini which looked reserved on her, as she had, as yet, little to fill it out.

I sat down with Candy and tried to raise the conversation above that of her standard chit chat. Candy revealed that she was stupid and often felt out of place when talking to intelligent and worldly people. Candy had long ago realized that her mother was beautiful but not very smart either. She had been her father's trophy wife until such time as she had left him because she had felt inadequate. I instantly felt sorry for Candy who believed that she had shortcomings in a world of seemingly intelligent people. Candy had realized that she was pretty, and like her mother, thought that she would use that to attract people around her, even though they considered her the traditional sexy dumb bunny portrayed in the Hollywood style.

I could see a little of myself in Candy and felt sorry for her as she seemed to live in a world that she could not fully comprehend. I was aware that beauty can be very advantageous for a girl in attracting a mate, but society can also be hurtful and want to punish you for it. Women who are envious of beauty, as they possess little to none themselves, can often try to undermine and ridicule those with it.

Joey had a double cabin to my complete delight and as soon as I was alone with Joey, I told him of Candy's situation and that I felt sorry for the girl who had been placed into one of life's categories, just as I had placed him in a category before I got to know him better.

Joey laughed a callous laugh which he was capable of, and then while still smiling said, "At least she is a beautiful dumb bunny which is far more advantageous than being an ugly dumb bunny." I was incensed at what was a callous statement as that also related to myself before Joey had forced a complete turnaround in my own character and intellectual capacity. I told Joey, more than asked him, to help Candy with her problems, after which I had other things in mind for Joey which would leave Candy's dilemma far from my immediate thoughts and needs.

Joey's alarm would go off every hour to check the boat's navigation and radar, as it was on autopilot which would have to be learnt to be trusted. Joey would soon slide in bed beside me again wearing only his boxer shorts. This gave me a new feeling of tenderness every time he slid back into bed and again placed his arms around me, even though I realized that it was mostly to warm him from his experiencing the cold night air.

The very next day, Robert asked Joey and me to keep him company while having lunch where he wished to talk about his daughter. Robert explained what we already knew, in that his daughter was very much like her mother who had played the sexy dumb seductress who had given him a child after which she divorced him and had left with a sizeable portion of his money.

Robert then said that his daughter was following the same pathway that her mother had, but he thought that Candy had the potential in life to fare much better than her mother. Robert then laughed by ridiculing himself, "Looking back I suppose; Candy's mother may well have been more intelligent than I gave her credit for, as she left with a huge chunk of my money for a minimum input of effort.

We all laughed but then Joey broke into his conversation as if a light bulb had lit up in his brain, "Tell me Robert; why would you employ a skipper as young as myself with only limited experience, to skipper your boat, while there are many more qualified skippers to be had."

Robert replied, "Firstly, I employed you, as you and Ashleigh are young and can provide a younger environment for Candy, in order that she may wish to stay on the boat for an extended period, but apart from that, I have a friend who is an old navy buddy and now a school principal, Ben Jacobs, who I went to with Candy's scholastic problems. Candy's results at school are not much more than disgusting and I asked him what could be done. You, son, are who he has recommended to help my daughter to improve her grades. He has told me that you are self-taught with only a year seven education and yet have tutored many of his students to improve their grades out of sight."

I decided to put in my two cents worth by saying that I was once a dumb bunny myself and Joey had helped me become an A grade student. Robert then took a fatherly approach with me and smiled as he replied, "Ashleigh, you are not telling me anything that I do not already know."

I felt as if Joey and I had been manipulated by Robert, but was pleased by that manipulation, as it had landed Joey and I on our first adventure and helping Candy had been my objective as soon as I had met her.

Candy was always eager to engage anyone in conversation, as seldom did anyone go out of their way to do so with her. Joey and I sat down with her on the rear deck looking at the smiling inquisitive face of Candy. Joey then asked, "Candy, do you know what color Britney Spears has painted her toes of late?" Candy, still smiling answered, "Yes, the color is iridescent spearmint green." Joey continued as if he were interested and again asked, and what color did she have before that?" Candy again replied, "Before the green she preferred sunflower yellow." Joey's smile disappeared and then asked, "Who is the president of Russia?"

A confused look appeared on Candy's face as she obviously had no idea who he was or even where Russia was for that matter. Candy was obviously confused as to why anyone would ask her such a question, as no one had ever done so before. Candy replied with a little shame, "I am dumb, and so nobody ever talks to me about such things; perhaps you should ask my father."

Joey then began his rhetoric with Candy which was not dissimilar to what he had once forced on me, "Candy, you are not dumb at all, but have just been forced into believing you are the pretty dumb blonde stereotype and so have become interested in the mundane so you can at least have something to say to others in your own stereotyping. How did you know what colors Britney Spears painted her toes?" Candy replied, "I read it in last year's issue of Cleo."

I then took over, as I knew where Joey was headed, "As you must realize, you have a fantastic ability to be able to recall such a nothingness item from a magazine from six months ago. Firstly, you must never take any credibility in such magazines as they are for entertainment only and most of the articles inside and including the covers should in all fact be classified under fiction."

Joey then asked, "Candy, have you ever read a book?" Candy then shook her head with her bright inquisitive eyes wondering why we had engaged her in such a conversation. I then asked, "Are you at all interested in love and romance and boys, to which she nodded in anticipation. I then gave her a Mills and Boon novel written by Wendy Marshall to read. I explained to Candy that this may be a good starting point for her to begin to read more than just Hollywood gossip, even though the author was perhaps a little too effeminate and girly for my taste.

I looked over to Joey who smiled at my attempt at humor and then took Candy's hands and pulled her head close to his, "Have you ever seen the movie 'Legally blonde' by an actress by the name of Reese Witherspoon?" Candy immediately replied, "Yes I have." To which Joey smiled and continued, "Well my dear Candy, tonight we are going to watch it again and you are going to realize that you are that girl in the movie."

I believe that Candy, for the first time in her life, considered herself more than a trophy wife's trophy daughter and she was beaming at the prospect of being taken a little more seriously.

It was only a day later when Candy said that she had finished reading the book. Joey and I again sat with Candy where we quizzed her about the contents of the Mills and Boon, Wendy Marshal novel. Both Joey and I questioned Candy about the contents of the novel and were surprised beyond belief as she answered every question that we would throw at her. Candy could recall every intricate detail down to what color knickers the girl in the story was wearing when she had discarded them for a moment of passion. Candy had a recall that I still longed to have, and so now we only had to make her become enthusiastic in paying attention to a more beneficial range of topics.

Joey had duties to perform which left me alone with Candy when I asked, "What other things are you Interested in?" It was perhaps because I took interest in Candy that she began to treat me as a confidante as she replied, "I am interested in boys and boys and more boys and am eager to be turned into a woman so that I can enjoy the pleasures of womanhood.

I could see Candy's future flash through my mind and realized that she was no different to me and that she wanted to begin with the last chapter of her Mills and Boon novel, just as I had wanted. Joey had thankfully slowed our relationship so that we would have memories to take with us into old age which I otherwise never would have had.

Candy's eyes related the fact that she was disappointed when I told her that she was trying to read the last chapter in her own book and that she had not even started writing the first chapter. This dialogue confused her until she realized what was being said and then replied, "You are sounding like my mother who wants me to restrict myself even though she obviously never restricted herself."

I smiled as I replied, "I mostly sound like Joey, as Joey had slowed me down so that we could enjoy all the chapters in our book in between the first and the last chapter. Your mother it seemed, read the last chapter first and that is why you are here." I then explained my story concerning Joey, in that I had wanted him very early in our relationship, but it had been Joey who had slowed me down and now I had far better memories and appreciated them better than I otherwise would have. Candy seemed wiser than her years when she replied, "I was not aware that boys showed any restraint, as my mother told me that men have no restraint at all."

I could not argue with that at all, as I believed that to be true in all cases other than my case with Joey, who had certainly showed restraint with me, as he was intelligent enough to know that I was ripe for the picking whenever he wished to have me. Candy then recalled the book she had just read and commented, "In Wendy Marshall's, Mills and Boon book, it was the young girl who wanted to slow down their relationship and the male who wished to progress further. I wish to find that type of boy and progress to the last chapter as soon as possible."

I was getting frustrated as my own book had progressed further, more quickly than I had wanted as I felt that I had a teenage daughter who had to be steered through life while I was barely older than she was.

I left Candy with her thoughts while telling her that I had another Mills and Boon novel for her to read. I went straight to the galley and found a razor knife and obtained the Mills and Boon romance book and cut out all the chapters after the first and before the last. I walked back to Candy but this time in the company of Joey where we sat with her and gave her the now thin book to read. Candy flicked through the pages and exclaimed, "All the middle chapters are missing."

Joey then again held Candy's hands and pulled her close to him, "This book contains the story of Candice Denning who has no chapters to her romantic story other than a beginning and end with nothing in between. Do you consider this book worth reading? It is like the story of someone's life that jumps from a birth to a death without anything in between.

This was too much for Candy who had tears running down her cheeks, when she softly spoke to us both, "I wish to find a boy who loves me and for me to love. A girl like me who is not very smart may have trouble in finding someone to love her and so if I find someone then I will try my utmost to keep him."

I was almost in tears myself as I could relate to her circumstance even if it was mostly unfounded. I hoped for Joey to continue and say something soothing to her, but that did not happen as Joey continued, "Candy, you are right in that you are not very smart, as if you have a mirror in your cabin and cannot see a beautiful young woman developing, then you are not only dumb but blind. Your problem is not in finding a boy to love you but selecting the right one for you to love him back. A university is a place to find a young man who can love you and look after you."

Joey then looked at me before continuing. "You cannot find such a person sleeping overnight on a beach, and so Ashleigh and I will help you improve your grades so that you can make it into university where many chapters can be written in the book of Candice Denning."

It was then that Candy's father appeared on deck and asked, "Candy have you been crying?" Before Candy could reply, Joey stated, "Candy is no longer with us. I would like to introduce you to **Candice** Denning who is a beautiful and intelligent young woman who wishes to be considered when meaningful conversations are taking place." Robert smiled as he replied, "I am pleased to make your acquaintance Miss Denning." Candice was beaming just at the thought of being taken seriously, which was as apparent to us as much as it was for herself.

The following months progressed, and schooling had to be done on board where Joey and I took turns in mentoring Candice, which was easy with the ship to shore link for long distance students on the home-schooling network. The books that we fed to Candice progressed from the Mills and Boon novels to more relevant books required by her schooling. Candice now showed that she had an unbelievable recall, remembering much of what she was now reading, which was obviously more relevant than the color of Brittany Spears' toenail polish.

It was over a month later when we were on our way back down from New Guinea travelling along the east coast of Australia that I was feeling happy with Candice's progress, as she was a very fast learner, and beginning to show great promise. I often sunbaked with Candice in the midafternoons and one afternoon I caught her crying. I immediately asked why, and she said that while on the boat she felt alone, as I had Joey, but she had no one. She said that she wished to at least be back at her school, even though it was a girl's school. Things would not be much better there, as even though she was in the company of other girls, she still felt alone.

I understood Candice's problems far better than she realized and that night I relayed the situation to Joey who seemed to listen but then went to sleep. It was in the morning when Joey woke that he said to me that he was overworked and needed help. I, of course, knew that Joey was far from overworked, and his statement remained a mystery to me until he said that he needed to employ a young lad about Candice's age to relieve him of part of his burden.

Chapter 10.
A Love interest.

Joey said that he had tutored a young student by the name of Jack some time ago whose wealthy parents felt indebted to him and said that if he ever required assistance in the future then to just ask for it.

Joey and I had breakfast with Robert while Candice was still asleep, when Robert was informed that his daughter was lonely and, in most probability, would most likely soon ask to go home. Joey also explained that he was overworked and required a navigator to lighten his load and had a boy in mind who had just turned sixteen. Poor Robert was confused and asked, "What qualifications could a boy of sixteen possibly have as a navigator?" Joey then smiled as he answered Robert's query, "His qualifications are that he is a pleasant boy and is sixteen years old." It was Robert who now smiled as he understood that the boy would provide the correct type of company to keep his daughter on board the boat.

We stopped at most ports along the coast and at one we hired a 'navigator' who was waiting for us. Joey had rung Jack's parents and explained that he required Jack to keep this young girl company as she was lonely travelling with her father on his powered yacht. Joey explained that Jack would be paid and that he would tutor Jack as he was already tutoring the young girl.

Young Jack came on board via the tender while Candice was sunning herself while reading a book on the front deck. Joey introduced Jack to Robert and me after which Robert left us sitting while enjoying a cup of tea. Jack immediately asked, "Where is this ugly duckling who I have to keep company with? She must be more than just plain for you to think that the likes of me will brighten her outlook."

Joey then, with his mischievous look that I was becoming accustomed to, replied, "This girl is not only ugly but is absolutely hideous, but you owe me and so you must repay the favor. Candice is on the forward deck, so go out and introduce yourself. Jack reluctantly disappeared through the door to the front deck while we looked through the glass window to see his reaction.

Jack stood motionless as he viewed the slim torso of the beautiful young girl reading a book. Candice looked up and asked, "Can I help you?" Jack immediately replied, "You can hold my hand and show me around this boat, after which you can keep me company for the rest of my life and become the mother of my children."

Candice was Candy again and her eyes increased in size as she stared at handsome young Jack who had already captured her heart with only a few words. Candice smiled and then took Jack by the hand and began to show him around the boat. I asked Joey, "Did you school Jack into saying those words?" Joey replied, "No, but I would have been proud of it if I did." I immediately realized why Joey had chosen Jack to keep Candice from asking to go home, for if I were in Candice's shoes I would never wish to go home as long as handsome young Jack was on board.

Much later Jack returned and sarcastically commented to Joey, "If you ever have more girls as hideously repulsive as Candice then I will happily again be at your service."

Both Candice and Jack were in year ten of school and so could be tutored together and could learn together, which is exactly what happened. I was teaching them both one morning when Candice looked up from her book and said to me, "I am already busy writing the first chapter of my own book." Jack then asked, "Candice, are you writing a book?" Both Candice and I laughed but did not reply to Jack's query, leaving him confused.

After a three-month period, there would be an end term test just as was had by other full-time students. Jack's results had been respectable for some time now and so all expectations were on Candice's results. Her results were received over the ship to shore computer link and everyone including her father was there when we all viewed her results.

Candice had received three B's while the others were C's. Candy had never in her whole life ever scored a B and now the eyes of Candice portrayed an acknowledgement that she may not be the dumb bunny that she had previously thought she was, but soon would be able to hold her own with more intelligent people. Candice hugged her father Robert after which she hugged Joey and me, after which she embraced Jack. While hugging Candice, Jack, without thinking in a moment of exhilaration, placed his lips on hers and kissed her.

Candice gave her father an embarrassing stare, and without emitting a sound, was asking her father if he had objections to such intimacy. Robert looked into his daughter's eyes as a father would normally do, and then smiled, which showed his approval. This was obviously a life changing event for Candice, for no longer would she feel as a disappointment to her father and to herself, and not only that but she had found a boy who felt strongly about her which meant improved possibilities on both facets of a girl's life.

A young girl always wants her father's admiration; a young girl mostly wants societies admiration, and a young girl certainly wants the admiration of a boy who she wants to admire her and love her. Candice now felt that she had all of the above and now wild horses did not have enough strength to pull her away from enjoying the ride.

Chapter 11.
My Protector.

The next months, we island hopped, every time visiting a new port of call and seeing the sights. On one island, Jack and Candice, Joey and I, decided to do the tourist thing and explore the island. We took the tender ashore and pulled it up the beach above the high-water mark after which we wandered for a while with Jack and Candice deciding to explore more of the village while Joey and I decided that we would take the bus tour around the island.

A 'bus' seemed as an exaggeration as it was more of an open truck with bench seats which could fit four people across each seat. Our bus driver and guide was a humongous islander who wore no shoes and had a smiley disposition. He greeted all the passengers, helping them aboard his bus with Joey and me being his first passengers. Joey walked down the side isle about three-quarters of the total distance and slid in and occupied the outer side position with me beside him.

The bus filled and I had a large biker type chap beside me to the right side with Joey to my left. This fellow had an unruly goatee and seemed smelly as if in need of a bath, but as the bus was open to the elements, it was bearable of sorts. Joey appeared oblivious to all the goings on, as his eyes were busy reading the tourist literature provided for the tourists.

We began to travel while having the driver speaking into a microphone situated near his mouth as he drove. We were travelling for about fifteen minutes when this biker chap who seemed twice the size of my Joey, placed his hand tightly on my leg just above the knee. I used both my hands trying to remove his hand from my leg but was not strong enough. I thought that Joey would have done something, but he only reached into his backpack to pull out a small bottle of his aftershave and a Bic lighter.

While I was still struggling with the biker-type person's hands, Joey emptied the contents of the aftershave bottle into his cupped left hand and reached around me grabbing the goatee soaking it in aftershave and with the Bic lighter set it ablaze. Joey's hand was also ablaze which he easily put out by padding it under his armpit smothering the flames.

The biker's hands were everywhere except on my leg as he was creating a great kerfuffle trying to extinguish the flames from his goatee. This disturbance had caught the driver's eye who immediately stopped the bus and proceeded down the back.

Without even trying to reason what had happened, the driver said that he was going to throw someone off the bus and was going to point to each passenger and when he got to the person who everyone wanted off the bus, he wanted the passengers to notify him. The driver pointed at various passengers until he came to the biker type with the still smoldering goatee and received a yes from the passengers.

This humongous islander-type driver manhandled the biker as if he were an unruly child, grabbing him by the collar and forcibly dragging him down the side isle to the steps. The biker was reluctant to get off, for which he received a bare foot to the middle of his back pushing him off and into the dirt outside.

I had never thought of Joey as my protector but now did. I had never felt as safe as I did that moment as I slid under Joey's arm and placed it tightly around me.

The passengers cheered and applauded the driver who took little notice and regained his seat and started the bus in motion and continued with his narrative as if there had been no interruption at all. Joey and me and Candice and Jack met up and later boarded the tender and returned to the yacht.

At dinner that night, I had everyone laughing, by telling and retelling the others of today's events. I believe that they all had a mental picture of this biker trying desperately to extinguish his goatee which was on fire. At the time it had been no laughing matter but now seemed that way. I slid into bed that night and all I wanted to do was hold on to Joey, my protector.

I knew that Joey preferred me to come to bed in my undergarments rather than my pajamas which I normally wore and so I decided to give him a treat and wore only my brassiere and panties. I then slid into bed where I held onto Joey as tightly as I could. Snuggling up to Joey, I told him that as I child, I always felt protected but later in life realized that my father could not protect me from everything and sometimes felt vulnerable.

I then explained that with him at my side, I would never feel that way again and asked if there was anything that I could do for him. Joey then said that the frontal clip on my brassiere was driving indents into his chest and asked if it would be too much trouble to remove the offending article. I considered that this was a minor request from someone who had done so much for me that day and so adhered to his request and again pushed myself into him.

I awoke to the sound of the motor turning over as we were apparently bound for another destination. On awakening alone, I picked up my brassiere from beside the bed to feel the frontal clip but found only round edges on the clip which would not cause any discomfort. I smiled as I pulled the blankets over me as I realized that my brassiere was only hindering feeling my bosom on Joey's chest and that he had lied to me for his own sensual pleasure which I must admit did not displeasure myself.

A few weeks later we were on our way to another island called Bougainville to the east of New Guinea where Joey and Jack were expecting good waves. Both Joey and Jack were avid surfers and so were always on the lookout for larger waves. When Joey and Jack went surfing, Candice and I, and sometimes her father, would go into the villages and meet with the local population, enjoying all that comes with being a tourist.

Joey and I were busy writing the next chapters of book number two in the life of Joey and Ashleigh, but I missed the uncertainty of book number one, when I was insecure in my attempts to seduce Joey, never knowing where I stood in his affection. Holding hands with Joey for the first time had been a humongous step forward in our relationship, not to mention our first kiss, or our ultimate experience waiting for the sun to rise in his sleeping bag when I had just turned eighteen.

I was perhaps unable to cope with a stable relationship and knew that the only way to revisit the chapters in book one would be to part with Joey and start all over again on another relationship with someone new. I was too levelheaded a girl to realize that such thoughts were ridiculously insane. I loved Joey more than my own life and wanted to grow old together with him. It was only now that I realized the importance of Joey's slowing down of our relationship so that we could experience all the chapters in between.

I would always have these memories to recall when I had any crazy immature urge to reinvent my relationship with Joey. We had taken another six-month contract on Robert's boat which was coming to an end when we arrived at an island called Bougainville, northeast of New Guinea. Both Jack and Candice were now excelling at their schoolwork, and it was only another nine months before Joey, and I, would attend the same university and start on book three of our lives.

Chapter 12.
A Lost love.

This unforeseen day started as many others had done before, where Jack and Joey usually had to wait until at least 10 AM before the surf was up, so we would often lay on the beach ourselves until such times that conditions were such that it made it worthwhile to go surfing.

Joey often lay his head on my lap when I was sitting looking at the ocean. It was this morning when I spoke to him about my innermost feelings in that I felt secure in our relationship and that I missed the insecurity of that initial period of getting to know one another. Joey just laughed at my statement as if I was crazy, which, I knew that I was, but never-the-less had such feelings. Joey then cut me short by saying that the waves were coming from the other side of the Island.

Joey and Jack then hired a vehicle to take themselves and their boards to the other side of the island and planned to surf there while Candice and I would walk down to see the sights of the village and perhaps take a tourist bus later to meet with them on the other side of the island. Candice's father Robert arrived at the beach and when we told him what was planned, he asked to come with us. It was in the afternoon that we all took the tourist bus around the island to see all that was to be seen.

We took the bus around the island where both Candice and I were looking for surfers on the windy side of the island. We eventually spotted their vehicle, but no surfers were to be seen, only two boards washed up on the beach. I was immediately concerned about sharks, but the boards seemed to be in pristine condition and so that did not seem likely. The bus departed, leaving us with the hire vehicle, after which Robert suggested that we walk up and down the beach looking for any sign of them.

At first there seemed to be no real concern, but as time went on, we were becoming more than just a little anxious. Finally, Robert decided to ring the police from his mobile phone, and soon after, we had two policemen with us who were as confused as we were as to their whereabouts. The policemen told us we should wait until nine o'clock that night, and if they had not surfaced by then, then to take the hire Mini-Moke back, and a search party would be arranged the following morning. The Mini-Moke did not require keys as it had a start button and an off button.

We waited until nine o'clock and then went back to the tender on which we travelled back to the yacht. We were all hoping to find them already on the boat but that was not to be. When we sat down for our late supper, all was solemn until Candy started to cry which started me crying as well. Robert tried some comforting words which were unsuccessful, after which we all retired to bed.

I had not slept alone for what seemed like forever and tonight that reality was forced upon me. During the night, my hand would travel over to Joey's side of the bed only to find him missing. During the night I thought of what stupid things I had said to Joey that very morning, in that I missed the insecurity of the beginning of a relationship. Was Joey trying to teach me a lesson? If so, then why would he involve Jack. It did not make sense. Maybe they were taken by sharks or killed during a robbery. These thoughts did not make sense, as surfers are well known to not have any quantity of money on their person and not worth robbing.

Early next morning we were again at the beach down from where their vehicle was parked with searchers already up and down the beach. About ten A.M. Ron, the police officer returned to us. He explained that they had not been taken by sharks as otherwise they would have found body parts washed up, as sharks are very messy eaters. He stated that they were most likely not robbed as a little money was still in their vehicle. Ron said that it was a mystery to the police as it seemed as if Joey and Jack had gone surfing and had never returned.

There was nothing left for us to do other than to wait and see if a body was found floating after a couple of days, which is common with drownings. Every day a spotter plane would take off and circle around the island but to no avail, and after some time Robert said that he would take us back to the Australian mainland where we would have to move on with our lives.

Every night I would lay in bed thinking that my brief conversation with Joey had something to do with his disappearance. I knew that Joey loved me like I loved him and so realized that this was ludicrous. Finally, the realization settled in on me that both Joey and Jack were dead. Even if Joey wanted to teach me a lesson, as he always seemed to do for everyone who needed a lesson in life, he could never have talked Jack into parting with Candice. My head kept churning up the possibilities but to no avail. Joey was dead; Jack was dead, and Candice and I would have to start our lives over again, and the second book of Joey and Ashleigh would never have an appropriate ending.

Candice went back to her mother after staying with Jack's parents for a week, perhaps trying to stay as close to Jack's memory as possible and to commiserate with Jack's parents.

What was I to do with my life now that Joey was gone? After days of crying myself to sleep, I was on my way home to my parents. I had decided to continue with my life as planned and go to university where I would eventually get over Joey and find a replacement for him; get married and have children with a new man in my life. This seemed to me to be the future which I had always desired, which now felt so very hollow to me without the presence of Joey in it.

I was soon back, living with mum and dad who both realized that I was in pain. After a month or so of obvious depression, my parents suggested that I should start dating again or at least go out with my girlfriends. I did plan to do more, and I finally found the courage to go and meet with Joey's parents. I did so one weekend when his grandparents also happened to be there. I had thought that they would blame me for what happened to their Joey, but this was not the case as they both hugged me as I was trying to apologize.

We all sat down to lunch when Joey's grandmother stated, "You are all talking as if Joey is dead. I would be able to feel if he is dead and I am telling you all that he is alive and breathing." Everyone at the table was shocked at Joey's grandmother's revelations and seemed to give it no creditability at all, after which Joey's grandfather also spoke, "I used to think that the old girl was a little batty myself, but she has been right too many times for me to discard her feelings so easily."

I placed no credence in Joey's grandmother as I had problems myself in relating to the fact that Joey was gone. I returned home and decided that I would prepare myself for university which was still five months away. Joey had already arranged his acceptance under the adult education scheme and had also arranged rental accommodation for us. I decided that I would still take the accommodation even though I would have to find another girl to share it with. I had a girlfriend already at university who was happy with the arrangement and so that was also set.

Chapter 13.
Life continues.

I decided that my life must go on and so I began to date again, which seemed easier and yet harder than before. I was constantly bombarded with requests from young men to keep them company which I did from time to time by going to dinner or movies or dances. They were mostly nice young men, but they were never my Joey, who may well be dead, but not dead in my feelings for him.

My friend's name was Kathy who was starting her third year of university and who had always been my friend. The lease on her old flat was up and the girl who she had been sharing with, had met a boyfriend, and had decided to move in with him, which left Kathy looking for a flat mate to share the costs.

I had been missing Joey for some time and was starting to realize that I was not prepared to go through life alone, and so decided that I would return to my initial plan where I would meet an ambitious young man at university and live happily ever after. It was one week before the start of university that Kathy and I arrived at the real estate office to pick up a key to our rental apartment and then headed to our new accommodation.

I had reservations walking up the stairs to our apartment, in that I had planned this momentous event with Joey and had lived this event in my mind many times over. Kathy asked why I had tears flowing down my cheeks when I reached the top of the stairs, but I gave no reply.

Kathy and I entered the second-floor apartment carrying our bags, after which Kathy asked which room was hers. I told her to choose after which she opened each door to look inside. Kathy closed both doors and replied with a smile, "I'll have the room that comes stocked with the young man sleeping in his white boxer shorts."

Could I hope that this was Joey, my Joey. I knew better, but who else would have been able to receive keys for this apartment from the realtor?

At first, I was horrified, but then began thinking, hoping for the impossible. I opened the door to find Joey asleep on top of the blankets. Joey was not dead which caused me to smile, but then I began to wonder why he would put me through such misery. I shook him awake and when his eyes opened, he only said, "Good morning.", even though it was afternoon. I thought that he was playing with me in reliving a past event but then grabbed my hand and pulled me to him and held me tightly.

I had a mixture of feelings. I hated Joey for what he had put me through, and I loved him because he was the love of my life. I was confused, as the Joey that I once knew would never have done such a thing. I returned

Joey's embrace while Kathy stood looking on. Kathy said that she would give us some privacy and go and check her own room to see if she could find one of the same, perhaps hiding under her bed. When the hugging and kissing concluded, my anger surfaced, and I began to hit Joey but was no match against him.

Joey then pulled me out of bed and said that he would make Kathy and me a cup of tea. Soon we were all sitting sipping on our tea when I asked, "Where the hell have you been?"

Joey explained that Jack and he had been hijacked by Malaysian fishermen who had forced them to do work on their ship which had been fishing illegally. They were never in any danger but still captives, having to work on the fishing boat. Mostly, they were made to do the cooking and cleaning.

Joey admitted that it had been an adventure for both Jack and him and even though they were captives, they were not treated as such and managed to have an enjoyable time that he would cherish for the rest of his life. I explained in no uncertain terms that this period had not been so enjoyable for me or Candy.

Joey confessed that they had eventually gained the confidence of their captors who had in general, treated them very well and had come to rely on them. Normally they were locked in their room when the ship came close to shore or to a port but as Joey was also their cook, he had drugged their meal one night when they were close to shore. When all the crew were asleep, Jack and he had put the boat on autopilot and jumped overboard and swam to shore.

It was that very morning that Joey had arrived, hoping that I would already be there, but when I had not yet arrived, he had fallen asleep. Of course, I could no longer be upset with Joey and so I stood and walked over to him and sat on his lap and kissed him.

I could see that Kathy was happy for me when she spoke to Joey, "I have heard much about you from Ashleigh, about all your achievements with only a grade seven education, but never in my wildest dreams did I think you capable of rising from the dead." We all laughed but then Kathy looked down at the floor and stated, "This means that I will have to find new accommodation for myself."

In unison, Joey and I told Kathy that she was welcome to stay as then the costs could be divided three ways, which would be of benefit to us all. It was then that I thought of Candice. Surely Candice could not know that Jack was alive and well and would be over the moon to see him again. Joey then explained that Jack was on his way home to see his parents while he had telephoned Robert and explained the situation to him, asking him to bring Candice and himself to have a celebration with Jack's parents, Joey's parents, and my parents, and to keep the fact that Jack was alive, a secret from his daughter.

Joey then explained that we should spend the night here and in the morning drive back home to where the celebration would take place. We did exactly that by talking into the night, with me hinting that we should retire to get some sleep for tomorrow's journey. I, of course, was trying to steer Joey to the bedroom without seeming to be too eager.

Kathy was wise to me and realized my intent immediately while Joey seemed oblivious to my obvious attempts at steering him into the bedroom, however, as soon as we were inside and the door was closed, I felt Joey's arms around me, kissing my neck like he had done many years before. I do not believe that I had ever discarded my clothing as fast as I did that day, ever before. I was expecting Joey to tell me to slow down to savor the moment, but he did no such thing.

Before having the chance to savor any moment, Joey and I lay panting on our bed with smiles on our faces after the consummation of the act of making love, even though, love had little to do with it. I awoke in Joey's arms which meant that I was in heaven again. I had thought that such happiness would never occur again and here I was with Joey, the love of my life, sharing a bed, sharing a life, and sharing the costs of the apartment in a three-way split with Kathy, or at least I thought that was the way it would be.

We had a pleasant breakfast with the only conversation being the occasional smile between us. After breakfast, we hopped into my car and many hours later arrived at Joey's parents' home where they were all excited to see their missing son alive and well. Joey's grandmother greeted Joey as if he had just been away and had not at all been concerned about his fate. His grandmother hugged Joey and stated that she could feel that he was always alive and well and so had not been as depressed as the others. Everyone treated her statement as the ranting of an old lady, but I gave it more credence than anyone else as I knew that a bond had always existed between Joey and his grandmother, from when she had taught him to read before he even went to school, which seemed to have affected his entire life.

This was a good part of my life, watching everyone come to life when they hugged their missing family member, and of me being treated as part of their family. After lunch that day, I wanted to show Joey off at my own home, which is exactly what I did when we went to see my parents. I had not fully realized just how much my parents loved Joey, as mother burst into tears when she hugged him. I could also see tears in father's eyes, which was probably more for the fact that his daughter's depression had come to an end.

Chapter 14.
Candy's Surprise.

I felt that all my ambitions and aspirations were coming to fruition but still had a hollow feeling. For a moment the cause of this eluded me until I realized that I needed to make Candice feel the same way that I did. Joey told me that Candice would be arriving by plane tomorrow in the company of her mother and that her father had already arrived and was staying at a hotel near the waterfront. We then went to meet up with young Jack at his parents' home, who was over the moon to see me, and I, him. I could see the anxiety in his features and could feel his anticipation in needing to meet up with Candice.

That night we stayed with my parents, and even though it was obvious that I had been sleeping with Joey for quite some time, I did not know how to make sleeping arrangements with Joey in my parents' home. It was my mother who without any moral restrictions said that she was tired and wished to go to bed, and that Joey could sleep in my bed with me. Mother then turned to father and said with a smile that he could sleep with her if he promised to be as nice to her as Joey would be to me.

What happened to my mother? It was that night that I realized that I was no longer their little girl, but a woman who would have access to all the considerations that a woman should receive. This was another hollow feeling that I would have to live with, as I had always longed for Joey to turn me into a woman, and yet was not overly enthralled that my parents no longer thought of me as their prim and proper little girl.

In bed with Joey beside me, my mind returned to when a young seemingly illiterate boy was hired to be my tutor and how my life had progressed since then. I remembered how Joey had slowed my immediate urgings in becoming a woman so that I could experience all the longings and expectations on the pathway to where I now was. I thought of how stupid I had been in being dissatisfied in wanting to experience those feelings again.

I realized now that those girlish uncertainties were part and parcel of being a young woman in obtaining a mate for life but was a hindrance to a woman who had found such a mate and should be savored as a memory in certifying what such a bond had on her life. Never again would I wish to go through losing a lover again, and I would learn to cherish the certainty of a secure relationship.

This night, I would remember the first time that I held Joey's hand in this very room; the first time that I kissed Joey in this very room; and the first time that I made love to Joey in this very room, even though that was only a wishful dream of a girl who hoped that Joey would have had the capabilities to scale a vertical brick wall to my bedroom window. I had Joey to thank for these memories, for understanding the basics of young people in love, as well as the implication these times would have on their future lives.

The previous night with Joey was a fulfillment of the lust that exists in all of humanity when two lovers have been separated from one another for some time, but this night would be even more memorable by holding onto my chosen mate and having him hold on to me. Never would I wish to return to pre-woman status ever again, and never would I wish to have Joey part from me ever again.

The very next day we had to meet Candice and her mother at the airport. This was to be a great day as I needed to be able to see the smile on Candice's face light up when she saw that Jack was alive and well. Joey and I picked up Jack on our way to the airport and met Candice's father Robert who was already there. We all had a plan as we all wished to experience the confused exhilarated smile on Candice's features when she would realize that young Jack was still alive.

It was soon that the plane taxied to the debarkation point when Candice and her mother arrived to find Robert and I there to meet them. I hugged Candice and she me and I was surprised that Candice's mother and father also carefully embraced. Together we walked down to the baggage lounge and retrieved the suitcases which there were certainly enough of. This had worked into our plan perfectly.

I looked shockingly at the baggage and then exclaimed that we would need manly help with them. I then looked Candice in her eyes and said, "This is too much luggage for us to handle. We will need manly help, and so I will go and find Joey and Jack and ask them to help." Candice had a look on her face as if I had lost my mind. Candice's mouth remained ajar but before she could mutter another word, I turned and wandered off. Poor Candice had thought that the stress of losing Joey had affected my mind. Robert, Candice's mother Sandy, and Candice watched me walk away.

In the distance I was soon returning with Joey and Jack in tow. Candice looked on as these silhouettes increased in size until we reached her, whereby Joey and Jack, without any greeting proceeded to pick up the luggage and place them on a trolley. That being done we all stood awaiting the expression on Candice's face. We expected great things from Candice, but Candice had disappeared, and Candy again stood in her place, who started crying. This action caused Jack to embrace her, and who started crying as well.

A few moments later there was not a dry eye between us when we were in the process of forming a six-way hug. We decided that all should be explained which we did over a cup of coffee in the airport cafeteria. Candy held poor Jack so tightly that I am sure caused him pain, but it was a pain that he had been missing for many months. What surprised me was that Candy's mother Sandy's hand travelled to her father's hand and held it which I could see was a shock to him.

All good things come to an end, and after explanations were complete, we had to leave the terminal which we did. Jack, Candice, and I, travelled with Joey in Joey's car while Candice's parents took a taxi. I was wondering what was happening in Sandy and Robert's taxi but was far more concerned about Candice who at this exact moment was again Candy, who I would expect would wish to proceed to the last chapter of their book that night. Speaking to Candy would be a waste of my time and so I explained my fears to Joey and asked him to speak to Jack.

Joey told me that while being captive on the Malaysian fishing boat, he had an abundance of time to converse with Jack. Jack fully realized that life should be savored and rushing to the last chapter in any relationship would forgo all the pleasures and anticipation in reaching that final chapter.

I now fully understood that Joey, my illiterate Joey, knew more about life than anyone else who I had ever met or heard about, and that he was always a teacher, teaching about life and how to avoid all the mistakes that young people constantly make, in wanting to fast-track their lives. Joey had slowed my life down so that I could experience all the insecurities and aspirations of finding a partner who I wanted to spend my life with. All the chapters in between our first and last chapter would never have happened, only for Joey's understanding of life.

As Joey sat beside me in the car with his outer thighs pressed against mine, I realized the stupidity of my statement to Joey on the day that he was hijacked, in that I wanted to relive all the insecurities and aspirations of dating. Having been without Joey for such a long time and finding him alive had brought on a complete turnaround in my emotions as I never wished to feel such insecurities ever again and would be overjoyed by feeling him beside me every night for my remaining years.

The following night, we all went out to celebrate the safe return of Jack and Joey. Jack's parents of course wore a perpetual smile as they had expected the worst. Joey's parents did likewise but his grandparents gave little away as Joey's grandmother had never doubted that he was alive and would one day return. Candice's parents, Robert and Sandy, were holding hands like teenage lovers who had found each other after a long absence, and of course Candice wore a continuous smile while holding tightly onto what she did not wish to lose again. As for me, I tried to hide my emotions which I found was not possible and so I also walked around with a smile, holding tightly onto what I also never wished to part with ever again.

This wonderful night came to an end when Joey came home with me where it was accepted by my parents that Joey would sleep in my room without reprisal from them. I looked back to only two years previous when I was ostracized for changing my clothes with Joey in my room and now it was accepted that he sleeps in my bed with me, not under duress, but with the blessing of both my parents.

Chapter 15.
A Step Back.

After an eventful night, it was again time to return to the two-bedroom lodgings near our university. It was a pleasant drive back to what I considered would be our home for the next few years. I felt more contented than any other time in my entire life and could not erase the memory of my last words to Joey before he was shanghaied by the Malaysian fishermen. How could I have been so immature in that I told Joey that I missed the adventure, the excitement, the apprehension, and insecurity of dating. I must have been insane, but that time was now past, and I would revel in the fact that I again had security in my life, but mostly in my love-life.

It was early evening when we returned to our unit and while we were standing at the door to go inside, Joey explained to me, almost with elation, that he had acquired accommodation with a friend who had another unit three doors down our hallway so as that we could adhere to my wishes, in that I could experience all the insecurities and apprehensions of dating again. I was shocked beyond belief, but not as shocked as when I found out that the other person sharing the costs of his unit was named Sandy who Joey said had been a longtime acquaintance of his ever since he had rented Sandy a room in his mother's beach-house.

Joey was never lacking in being able to understand the feelings of other people and yet he apparently thought that it would be acceptable with me for him to share his lodgings with a young woman. I had no reply other than to walk through my door and close it on Joey and then lock the door. Kathy was sitting in the lounge and looked up as I could no longer control my emotions and started to cry. I left Kathy sitting on the lounge while I went straight to my bedroom and cried for some time before Kathy came into my room with a glass of water. Kathy sat on my bed and asked what the matter was.

I explained that Joey had decided to move in with a girl named Sandy who rented unit eight, three doors up along our hallway. Instead of commiserating with me, Kathy just smiled as she explained that she had had the hots for Sandy for some time herself and that I should have no concerns. Kathy then continued. "Sandy is the nickname for Thomas Sanderson who is obviously not a threat to you." Tears were still flowing down my cheeks as I began to smile. I drank the full glass of water before I was again composed, and was happy beyond belief, when just moments before, I was sad beyond belief.

Kathy then left me to my own thoughts when realization set in that I had asked for this myself. Long ago I had wished to re-experience all the insecurities and exhilaration of dating but perhaps I should have thought it through a little more. I finally cried myself to sleep as I had found Joey alive and well, only to be again without any company in my bed at night.

I had had exhausting days and so I managed to sleep in a little longer than usual. I walked out of my bedroom still in my nightie only to find Joey chatting with Kathy and smiling when they saw me. Kathy had explained to Joey of my misconceptions about Sandy, in that I thought Sandy to be a female. In the past I had often formed untrue and misguided thoughts regarding Joey's possible infidelities with other women only to leave myself up to ridicule and today was no different. I ended up laughing at my own misconceptions of Joey and Sandy while enjoying a well needed cup of coffee.

At ten A.M. that day, we had to be at university for orientation-day where we would be shown around and supplied with a list of books to purchase for that year. Kathy and Sandy offered to accompany us, as they were about to start year three and so knew their way around the university. Both Joey and I were not so naïve as to take that at face value as that would allow Kathy and Sandy to spend the day together in each other's company.

Before we had left that morning, I had a conversation with Kathy whereby she explained that Sandy had been pursuing her for some time, but she was purposely remaining aloof by staying at a distance so as not to appear too eager. Being aloof was certainly never a strategy of mine regarding Joey, as he had realized early that I had wanted him in more ways than one.

After having been shown around the university and picking up our lists of books, Sandy and Kathy decided to leave us, which left me frustrated by the attitude of Kathy who thought of keeping up pretenses in that she was only marginally attracted to Sandy. As I sat having a coffee with Joey at the cafeteria I unwitting used the commonly used expression, "Those two should get a room."

As soon as I muttered these words, I realized what would next come from the lips of Joey as he reiterated, "Kathy and Sandy are just starting chapter one of the book of 'Kathy and Sandy' while you are wanting them to proceed to the final chapter of their book 1."

We both smiled as I realized that I had understood very little of the lessons of life that Joey had bestowed on me, regarding living one's personal life, after which our lives had taken a few steps backwards, mainly because of some unthought out words which were spoken by me so long ago. We familiarized ourselves with our new environment, holding hands as we walked along. I must admit that it felt good just holding hands but being who I am, I immediately wanted more.

The day came to an end when we were back in my unit where I asked if I could make Joey a cup of coffee, which he accepted. I had planned this return to my living quarters during the day and so I commented to Joey that I would change into something more comfortable before having our coffee. I had seen this scenario in the movies many times before, whereby the female would return in an outfit of very little material but supporting a smile. I returned in my black frilly panties with matching bra.

When I returned to Joey who was flicking through a magazine on the coffee table, I thought that I was the only girl in existence who felt the anticipation of seducing her partner. I had not had a lot of varied experience with the male of my own species, but what I did know was that the male would in all cases be actively pursuing the female in the hope to end up in her bed. The female would then reluctantly allow herself to be persuaded into doing what she had planned from the start.

That was never going to happen with my Joey who was perhaps one of a kind in that he had restraint, which I was always led to believe, was never a trait that was experienced by any other male on planet earth. I was making coffee while having these thoughts when Joey approached me from behind and placed his hands around my waist, after which I knew that coffee would have to wait. As I lay with my arms around Joey while we were catching our breath, I realized that Joey, was no different to my perception of any other male, only that his seduction process was similar to that of a female where a female would prefer the pre-seduction process to take as long as possible.

I lay holding on to Joey and realized that the entire day was spent in seducing one another by holding hands and accidentally brushing against one another, and to feeling an occasional arm around a waist, not excluding every word that was spoken during the day and every smile that was given, I had learnt a great deal today.

I was, however, back in heaven with the love of my life lying beside me while I was attending university for my betterment, and whereby I would find a partner in life. I, however, would have to modify these ambitions as I had already found my partner in life.

I awoke in the morning, still thinking these thoughts when I felt that I was again alone in bed and realized that Joey had ventured to his own bed early in the morning. I was disappointed by the fact that I was again alone but elated in the knowledge that I would have to start my seduction process of Joey all over again.

Joey and I began a routine where we would study by reading study books during the weeknights and on Friday and Saturday nights, we would go out and find entertainment after which Joey would spend the nights with me including waking up with me. Joey devoured books including any and every historical book that I had brought home to read. I was more than just a little satisfied with my life by excelling in all my exams and assignments. Joey always helped me with any shortcomings that I had and so it was as if I was always in the presence of someone who I could question regarding any study material that I found confusing.

Whenever my classes and Joey's would not overlap, he would sit beside me during my own classes as there were always plenty of seats available. This occurred a couple of days every week which I did not think that anyone seemed to notice. Peter Freshman was our main lecturer and one day in mid-year he came up to me and asked who it was who sometimes accompanied me to his lectures. I explained that Joey was my boyfriend and was also my tutor. Peter seemed amused at my reply but said no more of it.

It was weeks later during one of his lectures that he explained to the class that some weekends ago he had gone to a book swap meet and acquired a book called 'History repeats' written by an author who he was not familiar with. He explained that the author related old and new historical decisions which displayed repetition. He then emphasized that modern day politicians and military warmongers should all be historians and make all decisions based on historical recollections. Peter then offered to loan the book to anyone who was interested in reading it.

After the lecture was over, I caught Peter as he was walking down the hallway. Without my asking, he apologized to me, "Ashleigh, I have already given the book away for someone to read but when it is returned to me, I will let you know." I quickly explained that I already had my own copy and that I could loan him my copy if he needed another copy. Peter thanked me and seemed to mutter out load, "Now here is an author who I would like to share a conversation with." I was beaming as I said that if that was his wish, then he should follow me to the cafeteria.

I could see that this confused him, but he still followed me to the cafeteria where Joey was waiting sipping on a cup of iced tea waiting for me. As we arrived at Joey's table, I instructed Peter to sit down and introduced Peter to Joey. Peter instantly said that he recognized Joey from occasionally sitting beside me in his lectures. Peter then turned to me and asked, "I came here apparently under the ruse of meeting the author to the book in question which I immediately realized was not feasible. Ashleigh, why am I here?" Joey sat quietly as I was again beaming by explaining that Joey was the author of the said book."

Peter's mind was in a quandary and explained that Joey was far too young to have penned such a complex historical novel. I was already floating above my seat as I said that Joey was thirteen years of age when he wrote the book, which was because his father had bought him an old laptop and told him to write something.

Peter was disbelieving as he quizzed Joey about the book and received answers to what was inside the book and often Joey's reply included page numbers. We ordered coffees and I had no more to say as Peter was too engrossed in his conversation with Joey. Before leaving, Peter turned to me and said that I should bring him my copy of the book and then he would have it for the other students who wished to read it.

Joey feigned embarrassment but I could see in his eyes that he reveled in the fact that I was proud of him. From that day forward, during Peter's lectures, Peter often made reference to the book 'History repeats' causing many of the students to read it. Not realized by me, was that Peter was biding his time until Joey would again accompany me to my lectures and that day finally came.

Peter started his lecture by having a show of hands as to who had read the book 'History repeats'. Almost all of the people in attendance raised their hands after which Peter asked if anyone would care to meet the author. Without waiting for a response, Peter asked Joey to come down to the podium. I had thought that Joey may well have been embarrassed by this request, but this was not so, as he stood and made his way to Peter.

Chapter 16.
Self Inflicted Competition.

It was when Joey stood and walked down to the podium that everyone gasped, as some were acquainted with Joey, and all knew that he was not a history student and only kept me company during lectures. Peter then asked Joey to tell his students how it was that he came to write this book. Joey had them laughing as he told them about his thirteenth birthday party when he had a young girl pay him attention down at a beach and refused to come home for his birthday party after which his father had kicked him out. He explained that soon after, his father had bought him a laptop and told him to write something which resulted in the book 'History repeats' as he had always been interested in, and read about, historical events.

Peter then asked, "And you were thirteen when you wrote this book?" Joey just nodded his confirmation after which someone from the audience asked, "Have you written any other books?" Joey waited a moment before he replied, "I have also written the odd love story for the Mills and Boon romance book company under the penname of Wendy Marshall. I noticed that all the young men laughed but it was apparently no laughing matter with the young women who just sat silent.

All good things come to an end and soon Joey was back with me while Peter stressed the importance of reading and that great things can be achieved by anyone who puts their mind to it. I sat in my seat with my arm through Joey's and could feel all the eyes on me but perhaps their eyes were looking at Joey.

After the lecture had concluded and as we were walking down the hallway, a herd of young women wanted to talk with Joey but asked nothing about his book 'History repeats' but instead focused on the Wendy Marshall, Mills and Boon novels. I was quickly pushed aside and so I thought that I would leave Joey to his fate and go and grab myself a cup of coffee.

It was much later when I was on my second cup of coffee that Joey found me in the cafeteria. He purchased himself a cup of coffee and then came to sit with me. As Joey sat down, he smiled and said, "If I knew that would be the result of taking credit for writing a few romantic stories then I would have done exactly that, many years ago." I tried not to laugh and was not immediately capable of it, after which we both burst into laughter.

I was just starting to feel comfortable dating Joey again but now felt despondent as I realized that I had created this competition for Joey's affection by my own stupidity. I realized that I was my own worst enemy as I knew what every girl was now thinking, in that, if the opportunity arose, then they would pursue a relationship with Joey, my Joey. The reason I knew this was that I would do exactly that if I was in their position.

Months went by and I became a more popular with the female population until I realized that many thought that they could get to Joey by associating with me. What I fully realized was that Joey was no fool and he would be aware that most of the female university population would be at his beck and call. The only girl who I felt safe with was Kathy whose love interests had still not extended past Sandy. She had confided in me that she would soon allow Sandy to share her bed.

I could not believe what I was saying when I told Kathy that she should never rush into such things. What a hypocrite I was, because I had never shown such restraint myself, and here I was giving advice to Kathy, while Joey kept me company every Friday and Saturday night, and other times in-between when the situation allowed it.

After I gave Kathy that well-meaning hypocritical advice, I noticed that on that Friday night, when Joey and me and Sandy and Kathy attended a function together, that about two o'clock in the morning, both Joey and I could hear sounds coming from Kathy's room. Joey and I smiled as we realized that Kathy and Sandy had come to the end of book one of their lives, and now had to start writing book number two, as we had. I arose early to find Kathy in the kitchen while Joey and Sandy remained asleep.

While sharing a pot of tea, little was said between us, but sporadically we would break into smiles at one another. Kathy and I ended up speaking for a short time after which we returned to bed as after all, this was Saturday morning and there was still unfinished business to attend to. I slipped in beside Joey without waking him and just held him while I had the greatest of feelings in that Kathy was now a woman as was I.

Over time, Peter and Joey became the best of friends to the point that Joey sometimes relieved Peter when he was teaching the odd historical topic. Joey had always liked teaching others and liked lecturing on certain topics. Peter even managed to get the university to pay Joey, and was employed as a teacher's helper, which I never fully understood how that was at all possible, as he was also a student. Joey of course, as expected, did well in all his subjects and had already been approached by a company who wished to offer him a future position, even though he wanted to keep his options open.

Chapter 17.
The seductress.

What bothered me most was a student who attended my own classes and who dressed as I would like to, but I would be bothered by the slutty messages this would throw to anyone who cared to look in my direction. I suppose I felt some admiration for Jenny Page in that she, without concerning herself with the disdain of unacceptable behavior, would openly display that image to society.

My admiration of Jenny instantly changed, when one day, Jenny wore this low-cut blouse which displayed much more than it hid and moved her position to the front row of our lectures. When joey would give a lecture or book diagnoses, Jenny would always have a question or query to make Joey lean towards her to reply.

I always noticed that Jenny would lean forward when Joey approached, when she would bring her shoulders forward and together in order that her blouse would expose sufficiently down to her navel as Joey looked down on her. I would have liked to be able to do likewise but I was not quite as well endowed as Jenny and would never do such a promiscuous deed in public. Jenny was obviously trying to seduce my Joey and so I thought that I must do something to prevent her from being successful.

I liked Jenny before she tried to steal who I considered belonged to me and so when Jenny sat having lunch at the cafeteria, I sat down with her and told her of my feelings regarding the slutty, not so hidden messages she was throwing in the direction of Joey. Jenny laughed as if I were saying something amusing and replied, "Ashleigh, I believe that there is a saying that states that all's fair in love and war", as if that was going to solve my problem with her.

I left Jenny's table after looking at the bread-and-butter knife and considering whether I should immediately stick it into her heart or not, after which I saw Joey sitting at another table waiting for me. After I sat down, I realized that Joey was wise to the reason that I had spoken to Jenny when he said, "If you are at all concerned about Jenny's obvious attempts at seducing me, then you should perhaps wear the same low top so I can see down to the indent of your navel as well."

Joey laughed, even though this was no laughing matter, but caused me to smile as well. I, however, decided to do exactly that and stopped at the clothing store and paid top dollars for what amounted to a miniscule amount of material. I would never wear such an item in public but decided that I would wear it around my flat when Joey was there.

I arrived home and changed into almost the exact outfit worn by Jenny and had my normal cup of tea with my roommate Kathy. Kathy instantly looked at my attire and stated, "Surely you are not going to wear that in public." I replied with a smile, "This outfit is for wearing around the apartment for Joey's benefit only." I then explained that Jenny was doing her best to seduce Joey during lectures and so this was war.

Kathy laughed at my discomfort and asked, "Ashleigh, where did you get that outfit as I would like to get a similar one to secure my position with Sandy, in case Jenny sets her sights on what I consider belongs to me."

Sandy arrived to take Kathy to, I don't know where, which left me waiting for Joey to call in. As soon as I met Joey at the door and he realized that Kathy had gone with Sandy, we sat down for our usual cup of tea at the small round table. Joey, without commenting on my attire immediately asked me to lean forward and move my shoulders together. I knew exactly what to do as he was playing with me to imitate Jenny's actions during lectures. We never finished our cups of tea before Joey stood and picked me up and took me to my bedroom.

As we fell onto my bed, Joey asked, "Do you mind if I call you Jenny for the next few minutes." I immediately put my fist into his ribs after which he laughingly replied, "Ashleigh will just have to suffice, I suppose."

I could see that I had hurt Joey by punching him in the chest. This was only a playful gesture and should not have provided any discomfort, but it apparently had. Joey's eyes watered as he smiled as he tried to belittle the pain which of course gave him away. Joey would not talk about it and soon I had placed it in my long-term memory, only to be recalled if required at a later date.

Much later we again sat with our now cold cups of tea, when Joey commented, "Now that Jenny's seduction of me has reached a successful conclusion, you can feel more confident in keeping me to yourself."

After Joey left, I came to the same conclusion as I had done many times before in that Joey knew all about life and knew me better than I knew myself.

Everything was going fine in my life when I arrived home one afternoon. I greeted Kathy in the same way I always did by inquiring about her day, "And how was your day today, Kathy?", I asked. I had known Kathy long enough to know when she was upset, and Kathy was seething with anger. But why? Kathy looked me squarely in my eyes and asked, "How could you do something like that to Joey?"

Chapter 18.
A Girl's Reputation.

I had no idea as to what she was getting at and so I asked. Kathy replied, "Only a slut would do what you did to Joey, sweet loveable Joey. I, of course, asked her to explain herself to which she replied that she understood that I had a torrid interlude with Jack Rancher which had been explained to her in the utmost detail. I rebuked her by denying any liaison with anyone, and even though I had seen Jack previously, I had never given him even the time of day.

Kathy then told me that while in the lunchroom, she had overheard Jack explaining to a group of his friends, in detail, of a liaison he had with me whereby I had seduced him and had sucked the life's blood out of him in the most sensual of ways.

This was obviously not true, but I realized that true or not, my reputation of being a good girl would evaporate quicker than the dew of a midsummer day. It did not seem to be overly devastating until I realized that Joey would soon come to hear of it, and even if he believed even one word of it to be true then he would surely leave me. I instantly fell into a great depression as I could not imagine a life without him. Joey would soon hear of my interlude with Jack, as those rumors spread like wildfire through the campus.

Most mornings, Joey and Sandy would walk down the hallway to have breakfast with Kathy and me. I decided that I would tell him of the rumor of my liaison with Jack that would soon be the talk of the campus, in order that he would not hear it from someone else. That night I did not sleep well at all, as I feared Joey's reaction to this, even if it was unfounded.

Joey and Sandy sat down and when we were all sipping on our morning coffee, I blurted out with teary eyes that Jack was telling everyone at the campus that I had a torrid liaison with him in the utmost of detail.

If I thought that I would get a sympathetic reaction, then I was mistaken, as both Joey and Sandy just smiled as Joey said to me that Jack often explained his prowess with young women in the utmost of detail. Joey then said that Jack was planning to go into politics and had a powerful orator's voice which captivated his audience every time he would practice his oratory skills. Jack usually did so by explaining in detail a sensual situation with another pretty girl every time he had an audience. Joey went on to explain "And when has the truth played any part in politics?" Sandy then added, "Not one person on campus believes one word that comes from between Jack's lips but are always eager to listen to another episode of his with a more than receptive female.

Joey continued, adding to my embarrassment by explaining that he was hurt that Jack took so long to include me in his narrations to a receptive public. I was greatly relieved but still did not wish to be the subject of such narrations ever again, even though I would make sure not to miss any episode of him with another receptive young woman in the future.

This was a close call, as I had thought that Joey may have abandoned me by believing such gutter trash, but I, once again understood that not too many people could pull the wool over Joey's eyes, and that for no moment, did he even considered that I would have been unfaithful to him. Joey was correct of course as I never had any inkling to stray, but just as Joey and the rest of society, was not blind to the allure of others.

Every Christmas, the university would close for an extended period which would allow both Joey and me to use the time to trip around which we would do after spending time at home with my parents and Joey's parents and to visit little Katie who was getting older every year and sprouting into a young lady.

Joey seemed more than a little depressed when meeting up with little Katie who was not so little anymore and beginning to date boys. Joey was no longer my Joey but was portraying the characteristics of the traditional father figure who was worried about a daughter just experiencing her puberty years. Joey always had everything under control but controlling a puberty daughter was beyond him even though he had been excellent when dealing with myself at my past puberty stage. I tried to explain to him that Katie was an intelligent girl who was not to be underestimated and was far smarter than I was at her age.

I said that I would have a girl talk with Katie and instill in her the advantages of taking it slow and easy with boys and the advantages of experiencing all the facets of young love without passing any of the enjoyable in-betweens. What a hypocrite I was, as that had never been my plan, and now it was I who was professing the complete opposite to another.

I returned to Joey to tell him that Katie was far smarter than I ever was and in no danger of making an ill-fated error in her love life. This seemed to sooth the savage beast in Joey who now could breathe a little easier.

Joey spent a few days surfing as there were some humungous waves coming around the headlands. We had met up with Jack and Candice who had decided to spend some time with us as Jack also had a passion for surfing. They spent a few days with us but then continued elsewhere which left only Joey and me. Joey spent days enjoying the humongous waves while I spent my days sunbaking and talking to old friends.

Chapter 19.
A Confusion.

I must have caught the eye of another surfer as whenever the opportunity arose; he would go out of his way to talk to me. His name was John Jameson, and I must admit that I was taken in by his forceful and yet delightful ways. I supposed that it would not be unfaithful to Joey if I would toy with John by leading him on, as long as I kept him at arm's length. John was exactly the person who I had planned to meet at university and marry and have children with until I found a beach dwelling misfit who I had fallen madly in love with.

I should never have led him on as it was late in the afternoon and Joey would soon be with me again as the daylight was quickly coming to an end. Finally, John bid me a good day, not long before Joey appeared with his surfboard walking towards me. That night Joey and I had made reservations to eat at a seafood restaurant. I was glad that John had left, as me talking to a male stranger in the twilight hours may have been embarrassing for me and perhaps hurtful for Joey.

Unknown to me, during the day, Joey had caught some huge lobsters which were in a plastic bag for the chef to cook up for us. Joey had never ceased to amaze me, and I was content to sip on my glass of white wine admiring the young man who I would spend the rest of my life with, and who would be the father of my children.

As I looked up from my glass of wine, I saw John who was looking at me. I was now in a dilemma as I knew that my sitting with Joey would not hinder someone as determined as John. I decided to come clean and explained to Joey that a young man had been paying me attention down at the beach and had asked me to dinner and a movie. I told him that I had to respectfully decline as I had a prior engagement, but now, he was here at the same restaurant, and I was afraid that he may come over to our table.

There was a mirrored wall behind where I sat and so Joey asked me to point out the young man who asked me to dinner and a movie. I discreetly pointed out who this person was, after which Joey began his interrogation of me. As I never lied to Joey, I had to admit that John was the type of young man who I had envisaged meeting at university to provide me with companionship and future children but that was until I met this beach dwelling boy sleeping on the beach.

I was a little embarrassed by admitting that I had been attracted to John but not as much as when Joey turned and caught the attention of John and motioned him to come over. What was I to do and what was I to say? Certainly, Joey could not be upset over such a slight flirtation with another young man. Joey had never shown any signs of jealousy ever before and so why now? I trembled at the thought of what was to happen.

John came over and was motioned by Joey to sit in the spare seat at our table and as soon as he sat down, Joey asked, "Ashleigh here, said that she had met an attractive man down at the beach who had asked her to have dinner with him and take in a movie. Could that person be you?"

John was a little unsure as to where this conversation was going but still replied, "Yes that is correct. I met an attractive girl on the beach named Ashleigh and was attracted to her; the result being that I asked her to dinner and a movie in the hope of getting to know her better."

I was again embarrassed beyond belief. Was Joey insecure in our relationship? Was he jealous of my having spoken to another man or was he playing a game with me? Joey then leaned over the table causing me to think that he was perhaps going to hit John.

Joey then said that John should take me to dinner and a movie the following night after which we should get acquainted enough for me to make an educated choice between them. John said that seemed fine to him and that he would meet me the following night at a certain restaurant, after which we could decide on what movie to see.

After John left, I berated Joey for putting me in such a situation as I had no desire to have to break in another man, as I had already spent enough effort on the one I already have. I was trying to be humorous but received no smile from Joey.

We sat in silence sipping on our wines causing me to think of what Joey could possibly be up to, in doing such a thing. Joey always had purpose in everything that he did, but what purpose could he have in instigating such a scenario whereby I could end up in the arms of another man. John was the type of man who could cause a nun to discard her habit to reveal a scandalous bikini underneath with the purpose of seduction on her mind.

Did I want to have dinner with John? I suppose I did, but I was in love with Joey and would never want to be with anyone else, and yet Joey seemed to be pushing me into the arms of another. Was Joey putting me to a test? I was sure that could be the only reason but already had plans to turn the tide on his intrigue with a little intrigue of my own.

The following day I met John at the designated time and place to enjoy our meal. John was the complete gentleman. He spoke knowledgeably; spoke compassionately; asked about me and my life and what I hoped to achieve in the future. He spoke about his aspirations and that as well as being successful wanted to have a woman to love and to love him and to start a family with her. This was the man of my dreams before Joey came along and that dream was still my dream except that any dream would have to have Joey in it.

After dinner John and I took in a movie which was a romantic comedy. During the movie John placed his arm around me and kissed me. I could have rejected his advance out of hand but did no such thing as I wanted to secure another date with John to ensure that Joey's placing of me in this situation would come back to haunt him.

I allowed John to drop me off at my parents' home, knowing that Joey would be in my bedroom with a full view of what was happening in John's car. John kissed me before I left his car, after which I bid him good night. I walked into my bedroom to find Joey lying in his boxer shorts on top of the blankets feigning sleep. Joey 'awoke' and asked, "And how was your date with John?" I replied that John was always a gentleman, and I enjoyed it so much that I had arranged to have dinner with him again this coming Saturday.

I could see that my revelation put Joey aback and that was my plan. I wanted to over-shine any intrigue that he had in motion to make me come crawling back to him. I wanted to make him suffer. I didn't exactly know why but I knew that I was not going to let Joey get the better of me. It was like a game which I had no intention of losing. Joey opened the blankets to slide under himself and kept them open for me to enter as well.

I would normally cling to Joey as I was trying to sleep but this night, I put my back to him and feigned sleep myself, thinking of what Joey could possibly be up to. Joey never did anything without having a purpose but what purpose this scenario was to accomplish, I had no inkling of whatsoever.

I awoke with my head under Joey's chin with my arm draped around him. I tried my best to extradite myself from this situation as I could never hope to be seen to be aloof while clinging on to him. I eventually loosened my grip on him and his grip on me and stood to go down to make a pot of tea for myself.

Mum and dad often slept late nowadays and so I had the kitchen to myself until Joey came down and poured himself a cup of tea as well. After taking his first sip of the tea, Joey said that he was very impressed with John who he considered would be a good match for me if he himself were not around. What could Joey possibly mean by this? Whatever game he was playing, I planned to not let him get the better of me.

I knew that Joey loved me. That was not a factor which I would have to take into account and so I agreed that John seemed to be the best of people and that I was looking forward to this Saturday to get to know him even better. Joey then smiled to himself and suggested that we double-date on Saturday. The iris in my eyes expanded; my mouth was ajar, after which I asked, "And who have you got in mind to double date with?"

Joey explained that he would meet some random girl down at the beach and invite her along. For some men to make such a statement would be bragging as if such things were a certainty, but Joey had been absent from the beach only a few short years and his notoriety would still not have diminished and so I was certain that if Joey went down the beach and whistled, that a half dozen or so girls would rush towards him, trying to get to the first position in line.

As if it were no-never-mind to me, I said that it would be a good idea as long as he did not plan to do more than use her to double date. Joey's features portrayed a smile as he said, "Okay then, it is a done deal, we will double date this Saturday."

I sat sipping on my tea continually looking into Joey's eyes trying to get an inkling as to what he was up to. Could I have misjudged my situation with Joey? Did he love me like I loved him? I stood to place the kettle on the stove to keep it warm and on my return, while walking past Joey, he grabbed the elastic on my pajama bottoms and pulled me to him after which I was by necessity positioned on his lap. Joey then held me tight and kissed me with a tenderness, the likes of which I had never experienced from him ever before. Did this occurrence have any significance and if so, what? I was confused while savoring the moment.

I looked into his eyes and thought that I could see a tear forming but that was not possible as Joey never cried, and what would be the reason for this, and so I thought that I must have been mistaken in what I thought I saw.

Saturday came when John and I walked into the restaurant to find Joey with whom I would later find out was called Samantha, already sitting at a table for four awaiting our arrival. I was livid, as Samantha was beautiful with a figure that most women would kill for and of which I was already jealous.

I was mad with Joey as he could have chosen someone a little less glamorous with an outfit perhaps a little less revealing. To say that I was upset was an understatement and that was noticeable during our conversations. One could have sliced the tension with a bread-and-butter knife and that tension was obvious to John and Samantha. Finally, as the meal had ended and we all sat with coffees, John said that he wanted to see a particular movie after which I said that I had already seen it and so had Joey.

Samantha must have seen this as an opening to get away as she said that she had not, as yet, seen the movie and immediately stood and grabbed John's hand and told him to hurry as the movie was about to start. That was the last Joey and I saw of John and Samantha. I was still livid with Joey who just smiled at me and nonchalantly said, "Well it looks like it will be just you and me tonight, my dear."

I was instantly smiling at Joey who then took my hand while motioning the waiter to come and get his credit card to pay for the meal. Joey placed his arm around me as we walked out of the restaurant and with a laugh exclaimed, "I believe that I have been stiffed tonight as I have had to pay for the entire meal."

I was in heaven again as I knew that this episode was over, feeling Joey's arms around me where they belonged. What still confused me was the purpose of this misadventure, instigated solely by Joey. I would find out the purpose many years later in life but was content to put it into my long-term memory to be recalled later, and only if required.

The University years passed slowly with the attaining of my diploma in historical studies but what amazed me was that Joey had sat for all my tests and had attained the same diploma just as an amusement to himself as he loved to read such things as a pastime while even though I also loved it, I sometimes found it tedious.

Joey of course obtained his degree in electrical engineering, degree in chemical engineering and diploma in applied mathematics all done concurrently. I should have perhaps been envious of what was easy for him seemed so difficult for me, but was not, as Joey's achievements were also my achievements. I knew that Joey had been offered lucrative job positions with some prestigious corporations but was concerned that he often felt down whereby we would travel home and sit on the same strip of beach where I had once found this beach dweller, sleeping under a canvass high up in the soft sand.

I knew that spending time at the beach and sleeping on the sand would bring him out of any depression that he was in. It did for me as well, looking back. We both sat on the beach, looking at the morning sun's rays bouncing off what waves there were in the still ocean. It was then that I asked Joey which job offers he was considering. Joey then turned side on to me and placed his head on my lap and then said what I should have already known, "Ashleigh, I have been considering nine-to-five jobs for most of my existence. I even considered meeting up with Dolly Parton when she was on tour to explain to her that working nine-to-five is not my idea of how to earn a living."

That should normally have been an amusing statement, and it was, but also one that I should have been expecting as I knew Joey as well as I knew myself, or at least I thought so. I realized that it may take some time for Joey to consider where his destiny lay as he had many offers to consider while I had already accepted a job of teaching history at my old school as there was not an abundance of jobs on offer for aspiring history professors. I was happy with my occupation, as it was one that I loved, and a professorship may well come one day, even though I knew that day would not be too soon.

I sat on the beach with Joey realizing that while I thought that I knew all about Joey, I still did not fully understand him. I felt as if he was holding something back. For the first time in my journey with Joey, I felt secure that there was no other woman and that Joey loved me unconditionally, but there was still a mystery about him that I hoped would someday become open to me.

University days were now behind us, and I was comfortable relaxing before starting on book three of my life with Joey. Joey had always taught me to think of my life as a Mills and Boon novel and that is how it now was for me.

I knew that Joey loved me, but I was never comfortable in fully understanding this beach dwelling genius. If I were a genius myself then I may have understood him, but I was a mere mortal who followed the same guidelines of society as many others, and so my pathways through life would always be predictable.

Joey on the other hand was not limited to obeying society's rules and so his pathways were not so easily defined. One day I was having coffee with Joey and some friends at the cafeteria where Joey was always on call, and for this, still received free meals. Out of the blue, just after our friends left us, Joey said that he needed some alone time as he had a life's decision to make.

Chapter 20.
Lost Love, New love.

I was shocked, as Joey always had his life planned and now, he was insecure as to where his life was headed. Joey had never owned a mobile phone but buried messages in his lunchbox beneath the soft sand where I knew where to dig it up at any time with little effort. There was nothing I could say or do and so I told him to get in touch with me after he had made the decisions on his future. I expected that this would be over and done with within a week or two but that proved to be a miscalculation on my part.

Joey had disappeared again. The weeks went by, and I still had not heard from Joey. I contacted his parents only to find that they had also not heard from their son. I also looked at where he kept his groundsheet on the beach but found none and dug in the usual place for his lunchbox, but it was nowhere to be found. There had been an exceptionally high tide which had covered where the box was buried but the box should still have been there.

Without Joey in my life, I started work in February, teaching at my old school and again felt lost and alone. My mind wandered back to when Joey had disappeared from my life once before but realized that this time he was perhaps not coming back. Time went on and I realized that Joey had left me of his own accord. I began to socialize with friends and was of that age where I also began to date again. I had dated a few different young men, but all seemed to fall short of the relationship that I had had with Joey.

I was again living with my parents and even got into the same routine as when I was in school. I would jog down to the beach and along the hard sand near the waterline for a few kilometers up and down the beach every morning. I would always look for any canvass or sleeping bag perched high up on the soft sand but after a year or two, I realized the futility of my actions. Joey was gone. Perhaps he had taken a menial job somewhere after his decision-making about his future, after which he must have decided that I was not to be part of it.

I was beginning to take dating more seriously and was again somewhat content with my life. When I was jogging along the beach and saw a canvas up on the soft sand, I immediately surmised that this could well be Joey but when I walked up to the canvass and lifted a corner, I found myself looking at a couple of students who happened to be in a class that I taught and seemed embarrassed in that I had caught them together.

I wore a frown but that was not for any other reason other than I had hoped that it would have been Joey. This episode made me realize that I had still not gotten over the feelings that I had for Joey. I, however, never paid any attention to any canvass on the soft sand after that time.

I began on a horrendous time of dating, having everyone fall short of my requirements. I compared everyone to Joey and every one of them fell short. I was getting to the point where I thought that not one of these more than suitable men would satisfy my requirements of them.

I finally met with John again who said that he had received an anonymous letter whlch stated that I was again available for datmg. I was confused as to who would send such an letter but began to date John and as the years passed and I eventually thought that I had found someone who exhibited the qualities that were far more stable for my future than any other. This man of course was John who after bumping into me again and again at functions which were held at a nearby university, pursued me with a passion which I had never experienced before. John was now an instructor at university and had his life set out for him. We pursued the normal dating ritual but any restraint which was experienced by me with Joey was certainly not in John's make-up.

I found John as handsome, intelligent, and physically appealing as I had done years before. John was no Joey, but Joey apparently didn't want me, and a young woman needs a man to complete her and share her bed at night. I planned my seduction of John in a fashion where I would slowly let him know that I was ripe for the picking. This, however, was a waste of my planning for as soon as John received even a hint of my state of mind, our clothes were on the floor, after which we began on a ritual that had been absent from my life for far too long.

After our lovemaking if I may call it that, I felt as if I had been unfaithful to Joey, even though, fully understanding that it was Joey who had abandoned me. This feeling only lasted until John put his arm around me again, informing me that he was ready for much of the same. To have a man lay beside me was what all woman wanted, and I was no different.

I began to love John with a passion that had been absent from my life for some time. Here was a man who a woman could plan a future with and who would give her children with an assurance of stability. I thought that I had hit the jackpot with John and that certainly seemed the case for many years and with him, over time, had two wonderful children, both girls. I had always stayed teaching at the same school; jogged along the same beach; had coffee at the same coffee shops; and milkshakes at the same milk bar where Joey had received free food.

One day after my two daughters had become young women and left home, I believe that John realized that he had always had competition in the marital bed, as in my sleep, I sometimes cried out for Joey. John had no recall as to who or what Joey was, but of course his male ego would have been hurt as mine would have if he had mentioned another woman while sleeping.

I believe that this preyed on his mind when one day after our two girls left home to attend university, John sat me down while holding my hands and explained to me that he had decided to leave me for another woman who of course was younger version of myself. I was devastated but fully understood his predicament as I still had feelings for a ghost which he could never compete with.

Chapter 21.
Alone again.

We separated amicably and John paid for my share of our home after which he gently kissed me and said that he was sorry but could never compete with this Joey who surfaced every time I had a nightmare or a passionate dream. I, in turn, apologized to John and explained that I had always loved Joey as he was my first love but had never been able to extradite myself from my feelings for Joey, even though it was Joey who had dumped me. I tried to explain that I had always loved and been faithful to my husband as well. I then kissed John's cheek after which we parted to find new futures for ourselves.

What was I to do? Would I want another lover? I thought perhaps one day I might but was in no hurry to proceed on from where I now found myself. I decided to move in with my now older parents into my old room where I found myself jogging along the same stretch of beach where I found this beach dwelling boy over twenty years ago. I always looked up over the soft sand higher up the beach where I had first encountered and became enthralled by a beach dwelling boy, for what reason, I no longer knew.

Every morning I would go through the same routine by getting dressed in my jogging shorts ready for my run. While standing in my bra and panties, I would always feel Joey's eyes appreciating what they saw but when I would turn, there would of course be no one there.

It felt as if I was reliving the past by jogging along the hard sand of the beach. The shape of the beach had been changing over the years with the shifting sands and the never-ending tides, but I still remembered the exact spot where I had given myself to Joey that fateful day in my life. It was an exceptionally high king tide when I looked up to where the tide washed away some sand to reveal an old ground sheet wrapped around what seemed to be a square object inside.

Curious, I started to aid the waves of the king tide in uncovering the object that was inside the old canvass ground sheet, only to find what looked like Joey's old, sealed, food and drink container. I immediately pulled this up onto the dry sand and opened it to find a letter addressed to me.

I could not open the envelope fast enough to read the contents, which stated, "*Ashleigh, your life and my life must take different pathways from this point on. I cannot waste the remainder of my life with nine-to-five employment, and you cannot waste yours without such stability in yours. Also, from my birth onwards, I have had a degenerative heart condition which will limit my lifespan considerably. I wish to experience all that life can offer me for as long as I can and so we must go on alone from here on. You have allowed me to experience my first love, which in my case will also most likely be my last love, and so I must not hinder yours by remaining with you and slowing you down. Ashleigh, have a good life and remember me kindly as the young man who helped you with yours.   Goodbye. Joey."*

I sat on the beach the entire morning staring at the ocean with the odd crying session in between. Joey, I now knew, would in most probability have been dead for many years. I knew that his parents, sister, and grandmother who were all still alive would have known about him, only forbidden by him in mentioning that fact to me.

It was nine o'clock when I jumped into my car and took my findings to Joey's parents who viewed the package, but apart from that, said little to me. I asked if Joey was still alive or where he was buried and received only silence as a reply. It was only when leaving that I found a very old granny sitting in her rocker on the verandah when she motioned me to her to give me a hug. It was then that the old lady placed a note in my hand, unnoticed by the others.

Chapter 22.
A Happy Finale?

On the note was only an address which was well known to me as it was the same beach shack where Joey used to reside. I left Joey's grandmother and family and then went down to the beach shack, not knowing what to expect. Joey could obviously not be there and so I was mystified as to what I would find. I approached the veranda from the sandy side, again seeing some surfers of varying ages sitting looking at the ocean waves. I could not believe my eyes as an older Joey was one of them. The others had various alcoholic drinks while Joey sat with a cup of tea.

As soon as I approached, the others made excuses which left me alone with Joey who initially said little. I sat beside him and told him that, that very morning, the king tide had uncovered his note to me in his lunchbox from so long ago which I had only now found.

Joey explained that he thought that I would have found the note over twenty years ago as it was meant to be. I then asked how come it was that he was alive and well with his heart condition. Joey then explained that it was only recently, a few years back, that the damage to his heart seemed to have repaired itself of sorts, and with the aid of a heart implant of a pacemaker-defibrillator for safety was now again fit and healthy. Joey explained that he could surf again and do most anything. Joey also explained that he had always followed my life by conversing with his sister. I asked if he was aware of my separation and divorce to which he nodded acknowledgement.

Joey then looked towards the ground and asked what I was doing there, to which I replied with a smile, "I am now without any relationship and so I thought that I may find another illiterate homeless beach dweller sleeping on the beach who may wish to share my remaining years with me. Do you know of such a person?"

Joey's eyes searched for mine and then replied, "The young man to who you refer to, died some time ago and in his place sits a more stable middle-aged man who will take any tenderness that you have left in you, even if that has to be done in the remaining hours after a nine to five day."

What could I say or do other than to grab a blanket from Joey's old room and hold his hand and drag him the distance to where we watched the sunrise so long ago. It was midsummer which allowed us to again wake up on the beach. This of course reminded me of a time when my life had no meaning or future and I had needed the help of a beach dwelling boy to steer my life to give me direction.

I awoke to the cool air and the warm rays of the sun, holding on to Joey, the misunderstood beach bum, who I at first considered no more than an illiterate hobo going nowhere fast but had become the love of my life over time. I realized that my beach dwelling boy had given me the stable future that all females require but what he himself was not capable of. Joey was responsible for my having lived a life with two wonderful children and a stable ex-husband for many years. Those days were now over, and I was ready for any stable or unstable future that this beach dweller still had left in him. It was like de-jar-vu to open my eyes to the glare of the morning sun while holding tight onto Joey.

Life went on just as if twenty years had melted away. I was again a teenager and Joey was still Joey, a boy who I had never fully understood until later in life. I had wanted him to accept my ideas of life but now I had come to realize that Joey's outlook on life was now my outlook on life.

I took Joey home to meet again with my now older parents who were over the moon to see him again. This time there was no longer any embarrassment by having Joey in my room and now my parents knocked before coming into my room. This did little to quell my fears of being caught with Joey in an embarrassing situation. I was again a teenager who had a boy in her room who I wanted to make love to, but still feared that this would ruin my parents' opinion of me in that I was their reserved young daughter.

As the months passed, I introduced Joey to my adult girls and explained that Joey had always been the love of my life and not to blame their father for straying, as he may have realized that my heart was always elsewhere, even though I loved their father dearly as well. I told them the complete history of Joey and Ashleigh and how he had helped form my very being, after which they accepted him with open arms.

Joey never did have to work 9 to 5 as he received sufficient monies from his writings, and I had finally received my professorship and only lectured sporadically. Together we renovated the beach shack where we plan to live the remainder of our years together as beach dwellers. Joey had given me the stability that I had required during a period of my life, even though it could not be with him. I will now finish writing the story of Ashley and Joey and send it to the Mills and Boon romance book company, and will finish with the lines, "And they lived happily ever after."

Joey and I finally finished renovating his beach shack where we could appreciate the sunrises most mornings. My girls would often visit our shack, which they enjoyed immensely. I introduced them to Joey and over time I explained to them in detail who Joey was, and the complete details of how he had shaped my younger life and was responsible for theirs.

At first the girls were angry with their father for leaving me for another woman, but over time, I explained that he had felt abandoned by me because I still dreamt of a lost love from my past which he had no way of competing with. The girls reconciled with their father, John, and soon after, all was well between them. Happiness and contentment now seemed to be in everyone's future.

Chapter 23.
De-Jar-Vu.

Joey and I had been living in the beach shack for just over a year when Joey explained that he had landed another job as skipper on a powered yacht. I immediately suspected some intrigue and was right, as the yacht was the same one as we had been on years ago. It was Candice and Jack who had been taking Candice's parents on a cruise in their old age and were trying to relive their past. Jack had long ago married Candice and thought that they would like to relive their past, and to continue with an adventure that was cut short by being shanghaied by the Malaysian fishermen.

This time, the yacht was anchored in Aukland, New Zealand, where Joey and I flew to by plane. We were met on shore by Jack in the tender and then ferried out to the yacht where we met a much older John and Sandy who were soon to depart with their grandchildren to do the grandparent thing to a fifteen-year-old boy and thirteen-year-old girl. These were obviously the offspring of Jack and Candice, who had managed to raise a family.

We mostly stayed on the yacht while we toured around the North Island and South Island for over a week, after which John and Sandy and the children flew back home as the children had to attend school. This left Joey and me alone with Jack and Candice to tour islands to the north and north-west. While underway I was chatting with Candice who said she felt anticipation in a de-ja-vu sort of feeling in that something unfortunate could happen to Joey and Jack as had happened before.

I tried to allay her fears, but I had to admit that I also had such feelings, even though I knew that they would be unfounded. We were travelling to the Pacific Islands as we had done over twenty years previously and it was as if we had never had an interlude in between. We often sunbaked, saw the sites of the islands, and made love every day as if we were teenagers. Things went well for the best part of the year until we again visited the same island where Joey and Jack had disappeared over twenty years ago.

Jack and Joey had not lost their love of surfing and thought that they would try surfing again on the east side of the Island while Candice and I would spend time in the village. Candice and I immediately replied that we would accompany them and swim and sunbake on the beach while they surfed. We would leave nothing to chance in that Joey and Jack would disappear from our lives ever again.

We hired perhaps the same Mini-Moke as twenty years ago as it was neatly painted but obviously had been repaired and repainted many times over. We sat on the beach until the waves were of considerable size to entice the boys out to surf. Both Candice and I had not forgotten what had happened to Joey and Jack so many years ago, and so we sporadically had our eyes focused on the waves to find Joey and Jack who seemed to be miles out enjoying the huge waves. It was then that a vehicle parked near us, and four Malaysian men jumped out. Without speaking, they manhandled both Candice and me, forcing us into our own vehicle. I managed a peek only to see Joey and Jack surfing without a care in the world.

We had bags placed over our heads so that we could not see, but I could feel Candice pushed tightly up against me. Candice's hand felt mine and squeezed hard enough so that it now hurt. The only thoughts that went through my mind was that we would be sold on the slave sex market but that did not seem feasible as both Candice, and I, were around forty years old and not the ideal demographic for such an abduction.

I knew that Candice and I had kept our youthful figures and features but could still not understand where our immediate future lay. The car stopped and Candice and I were separated and dragged down another beach and forced into what could only be another tender. After a short journey we were forced onto the deck of a large boat, where our hoods were removed.

We stood in our bikinis but felt as if we were naked as the crew of the vessel gathered around us. Both Candice and I realized that we were perhaps not to be on-sold but perhaps only to provide sexual comfort for the crew. One older person came up to us and grabbed me by the shoulders and viewed me up and down and then spun me around and I imagined viewing me up and down again from the rear side. He just shouted a one-word command to one of the men and then did the same to Candice after he again shouted a one-word command.

This sailor disappeared and then returned with two long sleeved flannel shirts for both Candice and me which seemed to fit us perfectly. Things were looking up and what made it even more so was when the young sailor returned with long loose trousers which were tied around the waist with a rope. We had already been underway ever since we arrived on board and could only see the island on the horizon. We were relieved when we realized that we had been shanghaied to work on this huge fishing trawler just as Jack and Joey had been many years ago.

We were soon shown our duties, which included deck work, mostly cleaning and washing clothes and working in the galley preparing food for the crew. The crew seemed like hard taskmasters, but apart from that, were civil and friendly and often joked around with us. Candice and I bunked together and at night, wondering what, if anything, that Joey and Jack would be doing to find us or if they even realized that we had been shanghaied.

Joey and Jack had informed the police of our disappearance and suggested that we may have been shanghaied just as they were twenty years previously. The new police superintendent discarded this train of thought and did an exhaustive search of the island to no avail as we had vanished without a trace. Our men then decided that they would have to search for us themselves and so went down to the antique store which had an old cannon which was in working order with balls and powder.

Joey and Jack then decided to transverse the same course as their own shanghaied vessel had taken many years ago. It took a full month until a boat appeared on their radar which happened to be our fishing trawler. They pursued us, getting closer by the minute on the slower-moving trawler.

It seemed like we were on board for well over a month when we were aware of a great kerfuffle on board when the skipper had noticed the large yacht on the radar following them on his screen. The trawler changed direction which was always followed by a change of direction in the pursuing craft. There was little our skipper could do, as the pursuing yacht was capable of greater speed than we were and so would eventually catch up to us.

Everyone's attention was always looking over the stern to see if another boat was on the horizon which it eventually was. Soon the yacht became visible and to the relief of the skipper and crew, was not a police or naval vessel but only a large pleasure craft. Candice and I immediately recognized the yacht as our own but had a small deck mounted cannon on the bow. I had seen these before on worldly yachts, but they were very uncommon. Apparently, this yacht had made radio contact with our trawler and instructed us to stop so that we could be boarded by them.

Our skipper decided not to obey after which a cannon shot was placed across our bow from the cannon on the yacht which landed relatively close to us. It was now that our skipper must have realized that he had no choice other than to comply and so slowed the trawler to idle for stability for boarding.

Both Candice and I were in anticipation as to who would be in the tender, and I soon recognized the silhouette of Joey steering the outboard on the tender. Joey soon threw a rope to the crew on board which they cleated down and then lowered the ladder. Candice and I were directed to say nothing, which is exactly what we had already decided to do.

When Joey came on board, he was immediately crowded by the crew but pushed through them and walked over to Candice and me and asked how we were. I could notice that some of the crew were amazed at the brazenness of this intruder but what happened next was beyond all reason. The skipper came on deck and immediately smiled and embraced Joey who returned the hug.

Joey smiled, as this was the same skipper who had shanghaied Jack and himself twenty years previously. Joey soon explained that Candice and I were the wives of Jack and himself and if he wished to obtain more free labor then he had better look elsewhere as he would be taking us back with him.

At the start of each season, the skipper would shanghai a few people to do menial tasks on board and then mostly release them at the end of the season but sometimes kept them a little longer. This was of course a crime, but he had never been prosecuted for these actions, most probably because he had never been caught. The skipper's first mate was part of the original crew who also showed familiarity with Joey.

I felt as if I were living in the twilight zone where captor and captive seemed to be the best of friends. The trawler captain who spoke broken English said to Joey with a smile on his face that he was welcome to both Candice and me as our cooking left a lot to be desired compared to when Joey and Jack did their cooking.

After finishing laughing at Candice's and my expense, Joey then invited the skipper and his first mate to have supper with us that night on our yacht, stating that he would cook for them, which they agreed to. I spent some time in the arms of Joey after which we all boarded the tender and returned to our yacht. On boarding our yacht, Candice flew into the arms of an awaiting Jack who displayed relief over the safe return of the mother of his children.

All was explained to Jack in that this was the same skipper who had shanghaied Joey and himself those many years ago and who with his first mate would be coming for supper, as long as it was not myself or Candice who did the cooking. I was amazed that Jack also wore a smile which meant that he too, held no ill feelings for his previous slave master. Apparently both Joey and Jack had considered that their previous captivity was an adventure which they should appreciate rather than reject as a misadventure. These feelings of course were not reciprocated by Candice or me, who could still remember the heartache it had caused us both.

Jack and Joey helped with the preparation of the meal, which was not uncommon except for the fact that our guest had previously been our worst nightmare. The night went well with a lot of reminiscing and laughter after which our guests stumbled into their tender dinghy and returned to their trawler. We all sat quietly looking at the calm ocean and decided that all our previous adventures were coming to an end, and we would have enough memories to last us forever more.

Chapter 23.
Realization.

Many months later after our return I sat quietly with Joey on the veranda of our beach cottage. After reminiscing about our previous lives. Joey fell asleep allowing me to look at the beach dwelling boy who had changed my entire existence and given me everything that a woman could possibly need. He had given me an education; he had slowed down my romantic aspirations so that I now had memories of the expectations and uncertainties of experiencing first love; he had given me two lovely children who were by necessity not his own and a stability that is required by all females to raise a family.

As I sat looking at the ocean, I began to understand more of my life and Joey's part in it. As well as the obvious help with my education and restraining my immediate girlish urges, he had forgone his own loving future, to force me on a date with a good young man which had mystified me at the time, after which, when it was time for Joey to leave me to obtain the future that I desired, had written my future husband John, to inform him that I was again available for dating. His sacrifice had given me the life that I desired, perhaps even needed at the time.

Joey had watched me live my life from afar, knowing that he could never give me what I needed while expecting to have a short life himself. I only found of late, of what was his inability to sire children, because the pills that he was taking for his heart complaint inhibited the sperm production in his body. From afar, Joey had watched my two children being sired and born to another man. From afar Joey had watched me live a life which we should have shared between us.

To think that for many years I had thought badly of Joey for abandoning me, only to find that he never had. I sat on the patio with tears of compassion in my eyes for this soul, asleep, enjoying the little he required of life, which was to feel the ocean breeze on his skin while sitting in his boxer shorts looking at the ocean.

I noticed that Joey had not moved for some time and thought the worst. I shook the seemingly lifeless form, who to my complete delight, was only in a deep sleep and jarred awake. Joey then explained that he had been dreaming and wished to relive the past by wanting to sleep in his sleeping bag in the soft sand along the beach and see if he could coerce a young girl named Ashley to again share his sleeping bag. Let me just say to you, my avid reader, that sometimes in life, dreams do come true as mine did, with the help of a guardian angel.

The end.

Author ----- Gary Andy.

Made in the USA
Columbia, SC
23 May 2024

b6a33ce2-4d9c-42b1-9f9d-44759586bea5R01